Stopo
Sweetwa

STEVEN GRAY

A Black Horse Western

ROBERT HALE · LONDON

First published in Great Britain 1998

ISBN 0 7090 6224 9

Robert Hale Limited
Clerkenwell House
Clerkenwell Green
London EC1R 0HT

Photoset in North Wales by
Derek Doyle & Associates, Mold, Flintshire.
Printed and bound in Great Britain by
WBC Book Manufacturers Limited, Bridgend.

ONE

Jarrod Kilkline urged his horse to the top of the ridge. Once there he stopped to look along his back trail. There was a glimpse of movement amongst the trees.

'Oh hell!'

Lester Peabody was still there, following him. Not only following him but, despite all the tricks Jarrod tried in an attempt to lose him, catching up. The man seemed never to feel the need to stop to eat or sleep; with the consequence that Jarrod couldn't stop either.

Jarrod was a wanted outlaw, with a price on his head. And Peabody was a bounty hunter, although that wasn't what he called himself, who'd been after Jarrod since the New Year; almost five months now.

He wanted to take Jarrod back to Arizona to stand trial for his part in a series of stagecoach robberies down near Griffin Creek. At the time, Jarrod had been fooled by Harry Phillips, a Southerner like himself, into thinking that the robberies were being committed in the vain hope of financing another army of Rebels. They had ended in the death of a stagecoach guard and the realization that Phillips wasn't acting for the sake of the South but out of greed.

But however genuine his reasons, Jarrod had done wrong and he knew he would eventually have to answer to the law for it. He had long since given up on the hope of being able to return to Georgia, becoming a farmer again, or having any sort of normal life; especially with Peabody tracking him!

Lester Peabody smiled. It wasn't a very nice smile. He'd seen the furtive movement on the hill opposite and had no doubts whatsoever it was Jarrod Kilkline over there.

Peabody felt pleased with himself. He could never remember being so angry as when, several days earlier, he'd arrived at the Rock Springs jail in order to start out for Tucson with his prisoner, only to find that Kilkline had 'escaped'. He believed none of that. Kilkline had had the help of his sister, Ginny, and the Reverend Brian Tyler.*

Peabody had dreamt up all kinds of retribution to bring to bear on the citizens of the town. He hadn't bothered with any of them.

Instead he'd immediately started after Kilkline.

* See *Death Comes to Rock Springs*

The young man had several hours' start on him and had done everything he could to hide his tracks. It hadn't done him any good.

Peabody might look like an Eastern greenhorn with his derby hat, checked suit and shoes but he was completely at home in the West: an excellent tracker, good with any number of weapons and a skilful horseman. If people underestimated him the first time around, they never did again.

Now he'd almost caught up with his quarry and this time, as sure as hell, he wouldn't let him out of his grasp.

To his dismay when Jarrod reached the bottom of the hill he came to a wide meadow, almost bare of cover except for a stand of cypress trees and a few rocks. On the other side was another brush-choked hill that represented safety of a sort. First he had to reach it.

He glanced back over his shoulder. He couldn't see Peabody but he thought he could hear him, closing in on him. He had no choice but to cross the meadow.

Urging his horse out of the trees he dug spurs in the animal's sides. With a squeal it bounded forward and broke into a gallop.

And halfway across the meadow it stuck its foot in an unseen gopher hole. The horse fell forward and Jarrod, taken by as much surprise as his horse, somersaulted forward over its neck. He landed with a thump, the breath knocked out of his body and lay, stunned, where he had fallen.

Groaning, Jarrod sat up. And immediately saw Lester Peabody dismounting from his own horse close by. In desperation, he pulled his gun from its holster. Peabody was quicker, moving in on him, kicking his hand and then his arm, causing Jarrod to cry out in pain and drop the weapon.

As Peabody kicked the gun out of reach, Jarrod scrambled to his feet, flinging himself at the other man.

For a while they grappled together, punching and kicking. But although Peabody was a smallish man of middle height and slim build, he was also incredibly strong and knew practically every dirty trick there was to know.

He blocked nearly all of Jarrod's punches – and didn't go down when he was hit – whereas his fists seemed to connect with every blow. And he hit so hard Jarrod was knocked down a couple of times. Then he kicked Jarrod's legs out from under him. Jarrod had been left with a permanent limp from a wound received in the war and, white-faced, he lay gasping with pain before somehow struggling to his feet again.

Immediately Peabody caught hold of him, wheeled round and heaved him over his shoulder.

Jarrod found himself flying through the air to land heavily on the ground. Breath knocked out of his body he could do nothing but lie where he fell.

Peabody knelt on Jarrod's stomach, holding his opponent's two hands with one of his own. And from somewhere about him the bounty hunter pulled out one of his many hidden weapons. It was a derringer and he poked its barrel in Jarrod's eye.

'Been a pleasure to fight you, but you quit it now or I'll blow your brains out.'

Jarrod felt sure the man would pull the trigger. 'All right,' he muttered in defeat.

Peabody flipped him over onto his front and quickly secured handcuffs around Jarrod's wrists. He stood up, hands on hips, surveying his prisoner in satisfaction.

Jarrod rolled over so they were facing one another. He saw a man of about thirty-five, with dark-brown hair, so slicked back with grease that, despite their fight, not a strand was out of place, dark eyes and a face reddened by sun and wind. He wasn't even breathing heavily.

Jarrod was ten years younger. Tall and thin, his dark hair hung untidily about his shoulders. His eyes were wary and his mouth had a bitter twist of unkind fate about it.

'Don't you ever give up?'

Peabody shook his head. 'Very seldom, son.' He went over to his horse, bringing back a canteen of water. Taking a mouthful, he knelt down, holding it to Jarrod's mouth, letting him take a sip or two.

'What now?' Jarrod asked.

'I'm taking you to Tucson and you can make the trip either easy or hard on yourself.'

'I guess you're in charge.'

'That I am. Remember, there are three certain rules you need to abide by. Simply put they are do what I say, when I say it, and don't let the thought of escape even cross your mind. Follow them, that's the easy way. Try anything stupid and that's when it becomes hard.'

Leaving his prisoner to ponder his fate, Peabody walked over to Jarrod's horse, which had come to a halt a short way away. The animal nickered softly and Peabody saw that it was lame in the leg it had caught in the gopher hole.

'Dammit all to hell and back,' he muttered under his breath. Was nothing to do with Kilkline ever going to be simple? The horse could hardly walk. It certainly couldn't be ridden.

'You won't shoot it, will you?' Jarrod asked anxiously.

'Of course not. I'm kind to most dumb animals I meet. Besides, with rest it'll recover.' Eventually.

In the meantime what was he going to do? With only one horse, the journey out of the hills, let alone all the way to Tucson, would take far too long and give even a compliant prisoner too many opportunities to escape.

The only alternative was to head for the nearest town where he could either buy another horse or purchase two tickets on a stagecoach.

'Come on.' He hauled Jarrod up off the ground by his collar and shoved him forward. 'I know you've got a limp, and I suppose I didn't make your leg hurt any the less by kicking you, but you'll just have to walk for a while. It won't be for long, there's a stagecoach station over the next ridge.'

For a moment Jarrod wondered how Peabody knew all the things he did. He decided it didn't matter. All that mattered was that he was on his way to a bleak future and he couldn't do anything to stop it.

He started walking.

TWO

Just two passengers waited for the stage to Sweetwater Crossing.

Lately not many people had travelled to the town and hardly anyone came to the relay station. The room in which they sat had wooden planks for its floor as well as its walls. There was little in the way of decoration or furniture: just one long table with benches on either side, some chairs grouped round a smaller table in one corner, and a stove to keep the room warm. It was dark, too, with only two tiny windows and a couple of lamps that were, just now, unlit.

Unable to sit still any longer, Captain Myles Butler crossed over to the door and looked out. All he could see was the empty stage road and close-packed pine trees climbing the hill opposite. Above, clouds hung low in the sky, threatening rain.

The other passenger, a portly gentleman, who had introduced himself as Mr Marsh and his occupation as a dry goods salesman, said, 'I can tell you're glad to be returning home.'

Butler turned back into the room. 'I certainly am.' He nodded in agreement. 'I seem to have been away for so very long.'

And seen so very much.

'You fought in the war, sir?'

'Yes. For the North.'

When war was declared, it had seemed right – the only choice he could make – to volunteer to serve in the Northern army. Others said that what happened way over in the East was nothing to do with him. The war was far from Colorado where he had made his home. But his parents came from Pennsylvania. He'd been born and spent his childhood there. He believed in the United States of America and thought the Rebels were wrong in their attempt to break away. It was his duty to fight.

And after all it would soon be over.

That was some five years ago. Duty and patriotic idealism hadn't counted for much on the killing fields.

But now, at last, it *was* over. He would soon be home.

Butler was thirty-one. Tall and broad-shouldered, he was good-looking with brown hair, slightly thinning in the front, and blue eyes. He had none of the wasted look common to Rebel soldiers at the end of the war, especially those he had seen returning home when he served for almost a year with the occupying forces in Georgia.

As soon as he received his discharge papers he took off his captain's uniform and packed it away. Although he still thought he'd done the right thing, the war was finished and he wanted to forget it. Before he left Sweetwater Crossing he'd owned a small carpentry business. He wanted to start it up again, maybe even think about buying a farm.

Most of all he wanted to see. . . .

'Have you a young lady waiting for you?'

Butler smiled . . . to see Glenda again.

'Yes. Glenda Gardiner. She wrote to me all through the war.' He touched the coat pocket where he kept her letters. 'She kept me sane.'

He still felt the same about her as he had before he went away, still loved her and wanted to marry her; he prayed she felt the same about him.

At that moment the door opened and Floyd Fisher, the owner of the stagecoach station, came in with a bowl of stew. He was in his late forties, with a long flowing beard as if to make up for his bald head. He was accompanied by his sixteen-year-old son, Freddie, who was carrying plates and cups.

'Come and get it.'

Butler took his place by Mr Marsh at the long table. He didn't dare enquire too closely as to what might be in the stew; it might look like beef, but it certainly didn't taste like it. As for the coffee it was so strong the first gulp made his eyes water.

'When will the Sweetwater stage be here?' he

asked, when he'd got his breath back.

'Tomorrow morning. By rights. That is if nothin' ain't happened to it,' Fisher said.

'What do you mean?'

'Indians or outlaws.'

Butler raised his eyebrows at what he took to be a gloomy prediction that the stage could be attacked by either one. 'Is there much danger of that? I didn't see any sign of one or the other on the way here.'

'Used to have real bad trouble.' Fisher nodded dourly. 'Especially in the last couple of years of the war when both sets of varmints realized there weren't hardly any law around here and certainly no soldiers. Got real bold they did. Lots of people were attacked, killed. Stageline even had to shut for a while. No one dared move about the country.'

'Is it as bad as that now?' Mr Marsh looked as if he wished he wasn't on the way to Sweetwater Crossing.

'Nope. Fact, things started to improve soon as the war was over and they've gotten better since late last year when Fort Ludlow was established.'

'Fort Ludlow?' Butler had never heard of it. There hadn't been any fort in the area before the war.

'Yeah. It's over near Sweetwater Crossing, although it's far enough away the soldiers don't get into town much.'

Butler was glad of that. He didn't want Glenda tempted by any good-looking young men in uniform.

'Ain't much of a place. Hardly nothin' to it and it's only manned by a couple of troops. Serves its purpose though which is to keep the Indians in line. And while the army ain't responsible for catchin' outlaws, most of 'em are wary of causin' too much trouble too near the fort. But, yeah, we still do have trouble from time to time. This is empty country, mister, Indians and outlaws can cause trouble in it and easily disappear.'

Butler bit his lip. His journey from Georgia to here had seemed to take forever. Surely nothing could go wrong now, not when he was so near home.

'Don't you worry none, I'm sure everything'll be OK.'

With that Butler supposed he would have to be content.

'Now, folks, anyone for apple pie? Freddie made it himself, didn't you, Fred?'

THREE

'Stage is coming,' Harry Phillips announced, as he joined his four companions who were lying hidden amongst the rocks overlooking the road. He drew out his revolver, made sure it was loaded, put it back in its holster and stared, with a challenge, at Craig Wincott. 'Well? You gonna rob it or what?'

Wincott stared back, a bit apprehensively. 'I told you before, Harry, me and the boys are small-time thieves. We ain't stagecoach robbers.'

'Jesus Christ!' Phillips exclaimed, with an explosion of his easily lost temper. 'What the hell are you doin' here then?'

They were here because Harry had insisted and none of them had wanted to cross him. But now it came to it, Wincott knew he and the others weren't up to robbing a stagecoach. To do so, even for Harry, was to risk them all getting shot.

'It'll be too dangerous.'

'Christ! You said yourself hardly anyone travels on

this line. There won't be many passengers; there might not even be a goddamned guard. The stage has to slow here because of the sharp bend in the road and the slight hill.' He spoke as if Wincott was an idiot needing to be told these things. 'It'll be easy enough to get the drop on 'em.'

'And I said no.'

'What about you others?' Phillips stared at the other three members of the gang. 'What d'you say?'

They refused to look up. Scared they might be of Phillips and his unpredictable temper but, for the time being, they still agreed with, and owed their loyalty to, Wincott.

'Ain't nothin' to stop you robbing it on your own.' But Wincott knew Phillips wouldn't do that. Reckless and ruthless he might be; stupid he wasn't. He knew when it was time to cut and run.

Phillips strode up and down the small clearing, cursing and muttering. How the hell had he got involved with this bunch of no-good, lazy, useless losers? But he knew the answer to that.

Arizona had become too damned awkward, even for him, especially now he was wanted not only by the stagecoach company for robbing their coaches, but by the damn Yankee army for gun-running to the Apaches. It had seemed prudent to go somewhere else for a while and even better to do it hidden amongst a bunch of other guys who, as far as he could tell, weren't even bad enough to be wanted by the law.

But surely he could have chosen a better gang than this one? All they wanted to do was rob small trading stores and lone travellers; where was the fun or the risk in that?

Phillips was in his early thirties. He'd grown up on a large plantation in Louisiana, looked after by slaves; expected to behave like a gentleman, marry well and make money. He'd proved a grave disappointment to his family for he'd preferred losing money at cards, sleeping with prostitutes and behaving like the ne'er-do-well he was.

Bored with the easy life, the Civil War had come along to save him. He'd thrived on the excitement and danger and once it was over hadn't even bothered to go home. Instead, he'd ridden to Arizona where he'd carried on fighting and killing.

It was doubtful whether his family would have recognized him now, or wanted to. The once, at least outwardly, respectable and neat young man had gone forever.

He sported a scar down the side of his face, the result of an incident in the war when his opponent came off much worse. His dark hair was long and dirty, curling round his shoulders and he had grown a thick moustache. His eyes were a hard blue. He didn't care that his clothes were fraying at the edges, he wore them for comfort. A bottle of red-eye whiskey was rarely far from his side.

'Well, Mr Wincott,' he said sarcastically, 'if you ain't gonna rob the stage, what the hell *are* you gonna do? We're almost out of money and food. Perhaps you can discuss it amongst yourselves and kindly let me know.' Frustrated anger in every line of his body, Phillips strode back to where the horses waited.

Wincott watched him go with a little sigh of relief, wondering if there would ever come a time when the man would turn his gun on him, and fearing it only too likely. He risked a glance at the others. Could he trust them or would they side with Phillips?

After all, Harry was a colourful character – a Southerner who'd fought in the Civil War, a desperado wanted by the law, a renegade gun-runner. And he appeared to have no regrets over anything he'd done, but was proud and boastful of the fact that he was willing to shoot and kill to get what he wanted.

Wincott couldn't compete with any of that. He was forty-five and had lived all his life in the West. While he'd been in prison a number of times it was only for petty crimes. And he was not a violent robber, prepared to ride away rather than hurt those from whom he stole.

Of course, he could depend on his younger brother. Curtis would always stand by him and go along with whatever he said.

But what about the other two: Tom Ryan and Melvin Stack?

Ryan had just been released from a town jail down near the Mexican border, his fair hair still cut prison short. He was none too bright and was easily led. Melvin was just turned twenty and a cowboy, who, fired from his last job, was now anxious to see the elephant. Ryan was only an outlaw because he didn't have the brains to be anything else and Melvin only wanted some excitement before settling down.

Would they remain loyal to him or would they be seduced by Phillips's easy charm? And why should Wincott worry if they were? They'd been riding with him and Curtis for only a short while. He owed them no more loyalty than they owed him. On the other hand they were two good men.

With him they would never get rich – nor, he admitted, enjoy much excitement – but they would stay alive. If they joined Phillips, it wouldn't be long before, careless of his own skin, he got them both killed.

The stagecoach rumbled by. Unfortunately Harry was right. It was going very slowly and there was no guard. No one spoke.

When the dust from the coach's passing had settled down, Curtis said, 'What we goin' to do, Craig? I don't like to admit it but Harry's right 'bout one thing, we ain't got any money left.'

'Don't worry, I've got an idea.'

Curtis grimaced. His brother's ideas didn't always work out as they were meant to.

With nothing to keep them amongst the rocks, they wandered down to where Phillips and the horses waited. He sat cross-legged on the ground, poking about in the dust with a stick, a sullen look on his face.

Wincott didn't miss the fact that Melvin immediately went to sit by Harry. The boy was developing a bad case of hero worship.

'Well? You decided on our future yet?'

'We're near a town called Sweetwater Crossing. That's where the stage is goin'. Me and Curtis have been there before, ain't we, Curtis? It's got a saloon, livery and a couple of stores that trade with the ranches and farms round here.'

'So?'

'And it ain't got much in the way of the law.'

'So?' Phillips repeated.

'So, what I'm suggesting is that we ride in and rob the general store.'

Phillips flung the stick down on the ground and jumped up. 'Another goddamn trading store! What d'you hope to get from robbing that? Ain't you got no ambition?' He conveniently forgot he'd just suggested robbing an empty stagecoach and no one liked to remind him of the fact. It wouldn't have made any difference. Phillips always ignored his own mistakes.

'It's not just another store. It's bigger by far than any of the others we robbed on the way here. Ain't that right, Curtis?'

'Yeah.' It really wasn't bigger by all that much but Curtis felt his brother needed all the help he could get right now and didn't need him to disagree.

'And before we rob it we might get a drink or two in the saloon and maybe even rob that as well.'

'What about whores?' Melvin asked, his eyes shining. 'Does the saloon have whores?'

'Sure it does. Real pretty ones as well.'

Phillips snorted. He was sure that Wincott's idea of pretty wouldn't be the same as his; but, come to think of it, Melvin probably wouldn't know what to do with a whore anyway.

'I suppose your mind is made up? And the rest of you agree?'

'We've gotta get some money from somewhere,' Curtis said. 'And like Craig says we ain't likely to run into any lawmen.'

'All right. Why not? It should be easy pickings.' But while Phillips smiled genially, inside he was still fuming. A general store. What would they get from that? A few dollars, which would then have to be split five ways. He needed a good stake so he could head out on his own. He'd never get it if they carried on this way.

Still in a small town, with little in the way of law, you never knew what opportunities might arise to cause some mayhem. Phillips intended to keep his eyes open to seize any such opportunities should they present themselves.

'We'd better get goin',' Wincott said, going over to his horse. He wondered why Phillips had given in so easily but not knowing what was going on in the other man's mind could see no real cause for worry.

As long as they were careful nothing could go wrong.

FOUR

At last a break appeared in the pine trees. The slope of the hill led down to the road and it was here in a small clearing that the stagecoach station was situated.

There was little to it: a corral, in which some horses grazed, a ramshackle barn and the house, no more than a small cabin really, made of wooden planks nailed inexpertly together and sagging to one side. It had a covered porch in front, a privy at the back and an overgrown garden to one side. A thin spiral of smoke rose from the chimney.

Even so, Jarrod was glad to see it. His leg, where Peabody had kicked him, hurt and his high-heeled boots as well as the terrain were making walking difficult. Peabody hadn't set a particularly fast pace, at the same time he hadn't taken it slowly either. Jarrod was a wanted outlaw, his prisoner, and, whilst he wasn't a cruel man, neither was he going to make it easy on him.

'Stay put,' Peabody told him as they reached the corral. As Jarrod leant gratefully against the split-rail fence he dismounted, unsaddled both animals and slapped them in with the other horses.

He'd just finished when the door to the cabin opened and the relay station owner stepped out on the porch, rifle in his hands. He eyed them both for a moment then said, 'You a lawman?'

'Not exactly. Although Mr Kilkline is my prisoner. I've got the papers on him if you want to see them.'

'Not necessary. What's happened?'

'One of the horses went lame in the hills. I suppose none of your animals is for sale?'

'No. Wouldn't do you much good anyway, mister. They're draft horses, used to pulling the stagecoach; ain't no good for ridin'.'

'Pity. We'll have to wait for the stage. When's the next one due?'

'Tomorrow morning.'

'Where's it going?'

'West. Sweetwater Crossing. You can buy a horse there.'

It would have to do. 'Come on.' Taking hold of Jarrod's arm, Peabody led him inside the house.

'Name's Floyd Fisher. These two, Cap'n Butler and Mr Marsh, are waiting for the stage also.'

Jarrod looked at the man Fisher had called captain. He wasn't wearing any sort of uniform but obviously at one time he'd served in the army. North or South? Regular or volunteer?

'Just 'bout be enough room for you all. You can sleep in here. Won't be too uncomfortable. Will be warm. OK?'

Peabody nodded. He'd slept in worse places.

'Still some stew and coffee iffen you want it,' Fisher went on. 'Freddie get 'em some.'

Jarrod sat down at the end of the table. He felt awkward amongst these people, all looking at him, knowing he was an outlaw in handcuffs.

'He's not dangerous is he?' Mr Marsh asked.

Peabody grinned. 'Not now he's in my custody.'

'What's he wanted for?'

'Stagecoach robberies down in Arizona. At a place called Griffin Creek.'

Butler said, 'But you're not from Arizona are you?'

'No.'

'Somewhere East?'

'Yes.' Peabody had no intention of telling anyone any more than was necessary about himself or what he did.

'You're a long way from home.'

'Griffin Creek you say?' Mr Marsh asked. 'That's a coincidence. I was down there when those robberies took place. A bunch of ex-Rebs was responsible.'

'That's right,' Peabody agreed. 'Like many another they'd all drifted West when the war was over and instead of trying to start anew got into trouble.'

'Thought they were going to start up the war again,' Mr Marsh said. 'Can't think why they'd want to myself.'

'You were in the war?' Butler asked, turning to

Jarrod.

'Yeah, that's right. I was a lieutenant in the Confederate States Army. And proud of it too. It was my duty to protect the State of Georgia from Northern interference.'

'Georgia, that's where you're from?'

'Yeah.' Unlike Peabody, Jarrod saw no reason to be secretive. He was proud of his birthplace; besides, his drawl gave his origins away.

'Cap'n Butler was in the war too,' Fisher put in. 'Even though he lived out here and didn't have to go. He's been telling us of some of his exploits. Ain't that right, Cap'n?'

'Yes,' Butler admitted. 'I volunteered because it was my duty to help protect the Union. State's rights can't be more important than the Union.'

'What do you know about it if you lived out here and weren't even a Northerner?'

'I know you were wrong.'

Jarrod didn't like the way Butler was looking at him, suspicion and dislike in his eyes. Was the fact they'd fought on opposite sides, for different ideals, the only reason for the antagonism that crackled from him? Jarrod couldn't think of anything else.

He put his knife and fork down with a clatter. 'I wish we'd won.'

'You lost.'

'Yeah and ain't you Yanks rubbing it in? We'd have left the North alone if we'd won. It's a pity the North can't do the same for the South.'

'You rebelled and deserve to be punished.'

Jarrod went to stand up and Peabody pushed him back down. 'Be quiet. The war is over. You should both forget it. Especially you, Kilkline, seeing the trouble trying to resurrect it has gotten you into.'

'Kilkline?' Butler spoke sharply. 'And you're from Georgia?'

'Yeah. I said so didn't I?'

'I thought as much.' Butler sounded angry and stood up so suddenly his chair clattered to the floor.

As everyone looked at him in surprise he pulled his revolver from its holster and pointed it at Jarrod.

'Hey now!' Peabody exclaimed. 'What the hell is all this?'

'Mister, I was in Georgia at the end of the war and I happen to know Mr Jarrod Kilkline is wanted there for the cold-blooded killing of Corporal Frederick McLane of the Union Army.'

'Oh God,' Jarrod moaned, as that first fatal shooting, the one that had sent him fleeing to Arizona, came back to haunt him. He'd almost forgotten it amongst the rest of the trouble he'd found himself in.

'I'm taking him in for it.'

'No, you're not, he's my prisoner,' Peabody said coldly.

'A murder takes precedence over a few stagecoach robberies. And army affairs take precedence over civil matters.'

'Like hell. I haven't chased for months all over

Arizona and Colorado just to give him up to you.'

'Mr Peabody, I didn't kill anyone,' Jarrod protested.

'That's not what the Wanted poster says nor what I heard at the time,' Butler said angrily. 'You shot Corporal McLane down without giving him any sort of chance.'

'It was self-defence. There were three soldiers come to my farm. They didn't give me any choice.'

'That'll be for the courts to decide.'

'What, Yankee carpetbagger courts?' Jarrod laughed bitterly. 'What sort of chance do you think I'll have convincing them of my innocence?'

'It doesn't matter because you won't be standing trial in Georgia. You're coming to Arizona with me.'

'No, he's not.'

The argument could have raged on until it got out of control and Peabody or Butler shot the other, of which both looked capable. Floyd Fisher, fearing the same, stepped in between them, rifle in hand.

'Stop it the pair of you! Cap'n Butler put your gun away. Now! And you, bounty hunter, sit down! You too, son.' Fisher waited until they had all obeyed him. 'Now, I don't know the rights or wrongs of what y'all are sayin'. I don't wanna know. It ain't nothin' to do with me, but I ain't havin' a fight started in my house in front of my boy, where others might be hurt. Understand?'

'Yeah,' Butler said, while Peabody nodded, both of them reluctantly.

'Good. The stage will be here tomorrow morning. You'll get on it. By noon you should be in Sweetwater Crossing. That's where you can sort out your problems.'

Peabody glared across at Butler, but raised no more objections. He didn't believe this was happening. To have – at last – got hold of Jarrod Kilkline only for someone to come along to lay prior claim to him!

'It's late. We should get some sleep. Mr Bounty Hunter, you can lock Kilkline in the cellar. And I'll keep the key. That way none of us will have to worry about whether he's gonna escape during the night. And neither you nor the cap'n will worry about the other making off with him.'

'Good idea.' Butler cast a mistrusting glance at Peabody.

Clearly in a fury at this unexpected turn of events, Peabody escorted Jarrod to the entrance to the cellars.

'More trouble,' he muttered.

'I didn't murder anyone, really.'

Peabody didn't say whether he believed Jarrod or not. 'It doesn't matter. You're my prisoner and I'm taking you to Tucson. Don't you forget it. Go on, get on down there.'

'Don't I get any sort of light?'

'No.'

'Or a blanket?'

Peabody didn't bother to answer, he just gave

Jarrod a shove forward and closed the trapdoor.

Jarrod was left in the pitch black. Touching the earth walls, feeling his way, he went down the few steps into the low-ceilinged, cold room that served not so much for the storage of food but more as somewhere to hide in the event of an Indian attack. He didn't particularly care whose prisoner he was. He didn't want to be taken back either to Arizona or Georgia to stand trial where there could be only one outcome – guilty.

Miserably he settled down to a night sleeping on the cellar's dirt floor.

Harry Phillips lay awake, head resting on his arms, staring at the black night sky. As he so often did he was remembering the war and the glorious cavalry charges; Rebel yells guaranteed to put fear into Yankee hearts; the noise of guns and cannons being fired; smoke clouding the air; the shooting down of the enemy; men dying, their screams, never knowing the outcome of the day's battle.

It had been a grand time. Exhilarating, thrilling. There had never before been anything like it and never would be again.

Of course, while Harry had enjoyed the fighting and killing, he'd also believed in the cause of the South. He had continued to do so even after the South's weak and cowardly politicians had surrendered. The war should have continued until the cause was won or the last Southern boy had laid down his life.

Southern boys weren't afraid to die and they knew how to fight – unlike the idiots he was with now. They wouldn't have lasted five minutes in the Confederate States Army. God, they didn't even put out sentries on picket duty – any old Yankee could creep into camp and slit their throats.

He sighed heavily. The new regiment he'd recruited in Arizona had consisted of good men. With them he could have started up a new army and the South been revenged, had it not been for that bastard traitor, Jarrod Kilkline, the man he'd trusted to become his second-in-command. The only time he'd been mistaken in his choice of recruit, for Kilkline had sided with the Yank enemy. Had betrayed them. For such an act he would have to pay.

That was another reason Phillips had come to Colorado. He'd heard a rumour that Kilkline had also fled to the mountains. Phillips was on his trail.

And, by God, when he caught up with him, Kilkline would learn the penalty of betrayal.

FIVE

Sergeant Ray Cook rode into Sweetwater Crossing just as dawn lightened the eastern sky. It looked set fair to be another fine day, with a breeze coming down off the hills and the air filled with the scent of meadow flowers.

He considered Sweetwater Crossing a nice town, which was too far away, unfortunately, from Fort Ludlow to become a haunt of the troopers stationed there. The fact that if it did, it might cease to be such a nice place, was the reason why he'd left the patrol he was leading out by the river – much to the men's grumbling discontent.

The place served the few ranches and fewer farms in the area. Houses of varying shapes and sizes climbed the hillsides while below was the main square, lined with a general store, an outfitters, the jailhouse on one corner and a saloon across the way. Just off the square was the livery stables and stage-coach stop.

There was little more. But all the sidewalks were kept in good repair, being swept every day and, when it was wet, good-sized boards were placed across the streets so people didn't have to squelch through the mud and take that mud into the buildings.

It was obvious that Sweetwater Crossing's inhabitants were proud of their town and hopeful of its future; and with the area settling down after the war that future seemed assured.

Sergeant Cook was making for Ericson's General and Dry Goods Store where Glenda Gardiner lodged and worked. He dismounted in front of the building and tied his horse to the rail. Luckily it was too early for anyone to be up and about yet so he had a good excuse to walk across to the First Chance Saloon, which was open, and where, however early it was, he could buy a beer to slake the thirst he'd built up.

Glenda Gardiner stared out of her bedroom window, seeing the horse waiting patiently below. There was no sign of its owner and she wondered to whom it belonged. Could it be Myles? Her heart skipped several beats at the thought, but then she shook her head. If Myles was here he'd surely be banging on the door to be let in. Or she hoped so.

Did he still love her as he had before he went away to fight? In all that time she'd written to him at least once a month, but because of the uncertainties of the war she never knew if her letters had reached him. Nor did she receive many from him. And his words had been little more than short scribbles about where he was being sent or the outcome of the last battle. He'd never written about his feelings; not even after the war was over.

Glenda had hoped he would return to her then. Instead, he had remained in the army and had gone to Georgia to help in the reconstruction of the South.

He had written that it was his duty to do so, but maybe his delay in coming home was due not so much to duty but the fact that he no longer loved her – or wished to settle down.

Glenda had recently celebrated her twenty-eighth birthday. She was of middle height with a good figure and was good-looking with blue eyes and fair hair curling down her back, which, most of the time, she wore neatly pinned up.

She and her father had come out to Sweetwater Crossing when she was a child of six. Ten years later, her father had died and the Ericsons, who were recent arrivals, had offered her a job helping in the store and a room at the top of the house.

Not wanting to leave the town, she had accepted both. Whilst she liked the family and was grateful to them, she wanted nothing more than a family of her own. It seemed Myles Butler had wanted the same – until he went away to fight.

Promptly at six o'clock, Glenda unlocked the door of the store and stepped out onto the sidewalk, broom in hand. She liked this time of the morning when the air was crisp and clean and no one else was about.

Going over to the horse, she fed it an apple and patted its nose and just had time to notice the cavalry harness when the First Chance's batwing doors were pushed open and a sergeant came out. He was in his middle thirties, squat but burly with it, with bushy brown hair and a brown moustache.

He was making for her. Glenda found she was trembling. Something had happened. Something was wrong.

'Miss Gardiner. Glenda Gardiner?'

'Yes.'

'Sergeant Ray Cook from Fort Ludlow, ma'am. My commanding officer, Major Sanderson, detailed me to call on you to give you some news.'

'It's not bad is it?'

The man smiled. 'No, of course not. He wants you to know that Captain Myles Butler has resigned from the army and is on his way home from Georgia.'

Glenda let out the breath she'd been fearfully holding. 'Oh.'

'In fact, I wouldn't be at all surprised if he didn't arrive any day now, as the message about his return was delayed.'

That was the army for you.

'Oh, goodness.' Glenda didn't know what else to say or know what to do.

Cook smiled. He could tell that his news had both surprised and pleased the young woman and that probably she wasn't normally this tongue-tied.

'I expect you're looking forward to seeing him

again after all this time.'

'I am indeed, Sergeant, very much.' Glenda paused. 'But why did Major Sanderson feel it necessary to send you here? Especially since Myles er . . . Captain er . . . Mr Butler, has left the army?'

'Because ma'am' – Cook smiled again, – 'Captain Butler is a much decorated hero.'

'He is?'

None of his letters had indicated that.

'Yes, indeed. The army is very proud of him and his exploits and so should you be.'

'I'm sure I shall be, I mean I am. Oh, why didn't he write and tell me he was coming home?'

'Perhaps he has.'

Glenda nodded. The postal service out here was unreliable to say the least.

'And now, ma'am, if there's nothing more I'll go back and finish my beer.' And then he had to get back to his patrol, or the Indians wouldn't be the only hostiles in the area, his men would also revolt.

'Yes, please do.'

Glenda's heart was whirling, her mind was spinning; she felt excited, happy and fearful all at the same time.

Myles would be here any moment! What would she say when she saw him? What would she do?

She hurried through the store to the kitchen at the back where Polly Ericson was cooking breakfast for her husband, Colin, and the three children, Mary, the oldest at twelve, Jonathon, ten, and Eddie who was just turned seven.

'Come along, Glenda,' Mrs Ericson said. 'Breakfast is ready.'

'I couldn't possibly eat a thing.'

Everyone looked up in surprise. Glenda usually had a good appetite. Yet, nothing could be wrong for her face was wreathed in smiles.

'Whatever is it?'

'Myles is on his way home.'

'Oh, that is wonderful!' Mrs Ericson put down the plates she was carrying and went to hug the younger woman.

'He's evidently a hero!'

'In that case we must make sure we give him a hero's welcome.' Mrs Ericson began to plan in her mind what dishes she could cook for his return.

'Glenda had better help you, dear,' Ericson said, smiling affectionately at his employee, 'because it's quite obvious she'll be in no fit state to serve behind the counter today.'

SIX

For once the stagecoach was on time. Everyone was pleased; breakfast had been an uncomfortable meal, with Jarrod looking down-at-the-mouth and Peabody and Butler glaring at one another, hostilities likely to break out at any moment.

No one else was on the stage for the short run into Sweetwater Crossing. Peabody's horse and Jarrod's lame animal were tied to the back of the coach. After a cup of coffee, the driver climbed up on to his seat.

'Time to get on board,' Fisher said. He'd be glad to see the back of them all. Let someone else deal with their problems.

'Sit in the corner,' Peabody ordered, pushing Jarrod along the seat, squashing against him.

He sat next to his prisoner while Butler sat across from them. Poor Mr Marsh, anticipating an uneasy journey, took the corner furthest away from them all.

Jarrod, too, decided to take no notice of or interest in what was going on. He had the feeling Butler was itching to get into some sort of argument over the rights and wrongs of Southern independence, or wanted to talk about some of the battles in which he'd fought, maybe wondering if Jarrod had been in the same ones.

Jarrod wanted nothing to do with either. There was no point. He would never believe the South was wrong and Butler would never believe it was right.

And the battles were over.

'Ain't no guard,' Fisher pointed out, as he closed the door. 'Best keep your eyes open, although I doubt if anyone'll rob you this near to town.'

Peabody nodded. It was noticeable that this morning he wore a gun in a holster at his side openly. No one was in much doubt as to the reason why and it didn't have anything to do with robbers.

The driver picked up the reins and urged the horses into a steady trot.

Fisher watched it go, breathing an inward sigh of relief, then put an arm round his son. 'See what you get if you follow a desperado's path?' He was always scared that Freddie, alone out here, would get bored and take off for pastures newer and greener and, along the way, take up a life of wrong-doing. 'You're caught in the end, put in handcuffs and hauled off to jail.'

'Yeah, Pa.' Freddie had heard it all many times before.

'That there young man is goin' to end up in jail or at the end of a hangman's noose.'

'Yeah, Pa. Pa?'

'Yeah?'

'Who are they?' Freddie nodded towards five men who were riding down out of the trees and slowly approaching the relay station.

'Get inside!' Fisher recognized trouble when he saw it.

'Christ!' Harry Phillips muttered, as they reached the corral. 'Why the hell are we bothering to rob this place?'

'You said it yourself. We need money.' Wincott gritted his teeth, wondering why Phillips felt it necessary to argue with every decision.

'We ain't gonna get much here.'

'Anythin' is better'n nothin',' Curtis Wincott said, trying to keep the peace and feeling obliged to support his brother. 'And at least we can slake our thirst.'

Scowling, Phillips said no more as they dismounted, left their horses and went up onto the porch.

In the cabin, Fisher and his son stood over by the wall, shotgun and rifle in clear view on the table in front of them.

'What can I do for you, gents? You've just missed the stage.'

'Ain't the stage we're interested in.' Phillips took charge much to Wincott's annoyance. 'We want any money you've got.'

'Hey now . . .' Fisher objected and went to pick up the shotgun. He didn't make it.

Phillips already had his gun in his hand. Bringing it up he charged across the room, kicked the bench aside, leapt across the table and pointed the gun at the other man.

'Too late,' he smirked, reaching behind him to push rifle and shotgun out of harm's way. 'You shoulda had hold of the shotgun when we came in. That way you might have beaten me. Doubt it though, I'm pretty fast. Now, stand back and perhaps iffen you and the kid do as I say, then, perhaps, I won't shoot you. Otherwise, I'll take great pleasure in splattering both your brains all over the room.'

Fisher pushed Freddie behind him. He'd never seen madness in a man's eyes before but he recognized it now. He was very frightened, for himself, but more for Freddie.

'He means what he says.' Wincott confirmed his fears. 'Tom, Melvin, get those guns, take 'em away.'

He didn't want to give Phillips any excuse to shoot the man and the boy. In fact, he regretted the decision to stop here. They probably wouldn't steal much for their trouble and, with Phillips in the mood he was, it was looking as if Wincott's determination never to use violence on his victims was about to be broken. There didn't seem much he could do about it, except go up against Phillips himself, a thing he had no wish to do.

'Look, mister,' – Fisher stared at Wincott, trying

not to tremble – 'there ain't no money here. You're wasting your time.'

'Are you sure about that?' Phillips asked.

'Yeah.'

Harry swore. 'None, ain't there?' He pushed at Fisher, sending him sprawling. He stood over the man, cocking the gun and pointing it. 'Are you really really sure?'

'Harry! Stop!'

'Told you we wouldn't get nothin' here.' Phillips suddenly lost interest. Holstering his gun he drifted over to the window.

Freddie helped his father to his feet. 'Pa?'

'It's all right, don't worry.' Fisher tried to reassure him.

'Where's your food?' Wincott asked.

'Our food?'

'Yeah, if you ain't got any money perhaps you've got some supplies we can take.'

'Ain't much, but you can take it all.'

Phillips nodded. 'Don't fret, we will. C'mon Tom, Melv, let's see what there is.'

Curtis wandered over to where his brother stood by the door. 'I don't like this.'

'You think I do?'

'Harry is on the edge.'

'Yeah, and likely to go over at any minute and take us with him. Look, Curtis, let's get to Sweetwater Crossing, see what happens there and then go on to Utah like we planned, where we can ditch Harry. The other two can go with him or stay with us, whatever they decide. What d'you say?'

'Sounds OK to me.'

'Hey, what are you two plotting?' Phillips came back into the room, carrying some jars, followed by Ryan and Melvin also laden with supplies from Fisher's cupboards.

'Nothin'. We ain't plotting nothin'.'

'Good. I wouldn't like it iffen you were. Let's go. Hey, ol' man, next time we come through you'd better have some money ready for us or I won't act so nicely.' Laughing, Phillips went out of the door, followed by the rest of the gang.

Wincott glanced back once and shrugged as if to say he was sorry.

Once they'd gone, Fisher picked up the overturned bench and collapsed down on it, putting his head in his hands. He knew he and Freddie had had a lucky escape – had thought they were surely going to die – for if that madman had decided to shoot them no one would have been able to stop him.

Freddie put an arm around his father's shoulders and Fisher looked up to see tears in the boy's eyes. He patted Freddie's hand. Violence of one sort or another was all around them, but had never before entered their lives.

'Don't worry, Freddie, they've gone. It's all right.'

'He said they'd come back.'

'They won't. But, by Christ, iffen they do we'll be ready for 'em. Remember, Son, sometimes it's OK to shoot first and ask any damn questions after the smoke has cleared.'

'Yeah, Pa.'

'Go see what they've left us with.' As Freddie did as he was told, Fisher crossed over to the door and looked out to make sure the gang had gone. There was no sign of them. Even so he shut the door and put the bar across it.

Where had they come from? Where were they going? He thought he'd heard the oldest man mention Sweetwater Crossing.

Should he send Freddie into town to warn the townsfolk? The trouble with that was the gang would get there before Freddie and the only law in Sweetwater was an inept deputy, who wouldn't be able to handle a gang of thieves, however much warning he got.

But he felt he ought to do something.

Maybe Freddie could ride to Fort Ludlow. There he could warn Major Sanderson about the thieves and perhaps the major would send out some of his troopers to look for them.

SEVEN

Glenda stood in the doorway of the general store, twisting her hands together in nervous anticipation. The stagecoach was due at any moment. Would Myles be on it or would she have to wait another day?

'Won't be long now,' Myles Butler spoke eagerly. He leaned forward in his seat, staring out of the stagecoach window. 'Just round the next bend.'

The stage slowed to take the curve in the road and then slowed even more as the first buildings of Sweetwater Crossing came into view. A couple of minutes later, the driver steered the horses into the yard at the rear of the livery stable and pulled to a halt.

Butler was the first out. He was home at last! And Sweetwater Crossing didn't look much different to how it had when he left. Larger, with several more buildings, cleaner maybe, with an air of doing well. But home.

Mr Marsh collected his bag, nodded to his travelling companions and hurried away, anxious to find more congenial company.

'We'd better get on over to the jailhouse,' Peabody said. 'Lock Kilkline up and talk to the law. I'll come back later to see to the horses.'

With Peabody on one side of Jarrod and Butler on the other, they walked through the livery stable, out on to the street and Butler pointed to the jailhouse.

'Myles! Myles!'

He swivelled round. 'Glenda!'

A young woman was running towards them. Butler put his arms out and she ran into them. They hugged and kissed, much to the amusement of several onlookers.

'Oh, Myles, I've missed you so.' Glenda stepped back, suddenly pink-cheeked and shy.

'You too, sweetheart. . . .' Butler hugged her again. He wanted nothing more than to go somewhere private with her, kiss her, hold her to him, catch up on all that had happened while he'd been away. Unfortunately, there was Jarrod Kilkline and Peabody to consider. That little matter had to be sorted out first. He glanced back at the two men who stood watching.

'What's the matter?' Glenda asked. For the first time she noticed Peabody, a strange gentleman in his Eastern type clothes, and his prisoner, a young man in handcuffs. What had they got to do with Myles? 'Who are they?'

Butler put his hands on Glenda's shoulders. 'Mr

Peabody and I are in disagreement over Mr Kilkline. You see, Kilkline's wanted for a crime against the US Army but Mr Peabody believes otherwise. I've got to settle it for good and all.'

'Oh I see. But I thought. . . .' Glenda broke off. What could she say? That she'd hoped all he would want was to be with her? She swallowed her words. For Myles had that look of determined duty on his face that she remembered so well from so many years ago.

'Don't look disappointed, sweetheart. This won't take but a few moments. I shan't be happy until it's done but once it is I'll come back to you and we can be together. Are you still working for Mr Ericson at his store?'

'Yes.'

'Then I'll join you there in a short while. I'll be as quick as I can. I promise.' Butler kissed her again, then turned back to Jarrod and Peabody. 'Come on.' He was aware of Glenda watching him as he walked away. This was not how he'd imagined his homecoming.

Deputy Jim Newley looked up as the three men came into his office. Now what? Newley was fat and lazy and had only taken the job at his wife's urgings. Well paid and easy work, she'd said, and so far she had been proved right. He had little to do but collect taxes and round up the occasional Saturday-night drunk. He'd never been involved with really bad men and didn't want to be either.

He listened, frown on his face, as Butler explained

the situation to him, not really understanding any of it. He'd never been further East than Denver, never seen a black man, let alone a slave, and had no idea of what States rights meant. And as for robbing stage-coaches . . . well, he was only the town deputy, and if any robberies took place outside of town limits it didn't concern him, let alone if they took place far away in Arizona.

Vigorously, he scratched his head, frowned some more, then said, 'Well, sir, I ain't rightly equipped to say who's right or who's wrong. I reckon that'd be up to Sheriff Beale.'

'So where is Sheriff Beale?' Peabody asked. 'Can we speak to him?'

'I can't rightly say where he is. He don't often come here. Say about once a month.'

'When's he due?'

Newley frowned again. 'I don't rightly know. Couple of weeks. Mebbe.'

'Isn't there any way you can get in touch with him?'

'Nope.'

Peabody sighed. This was getting them nowhere. 'What do you do if there's trouble here?'

'Dunno. There ain't never been no real bad trouble. Nothin' I can't handle anyhow.'

Peabody thought that probably wouldn't amount to much.

Butler must have agreed for he said, 'Have you at least got a cell where you can lock the prisoner up?'

' 'Course.'

'Look, Butler, I'm not about to wait around here for a sheriff who might or might not arrive in two weeks' time,' Peabody began angrily.

'I don't want to wait that long either,' Butler agreed. He was anxious to get this sorted out so he could get on with the life to which he'd dreamt of returning. 'But we haven't any choice. This is too important for either of us to deal with. We'll leave him in your safe hands, Deputy.'

Newley looked as if he realized Butler wasn't paying him any sort of compliment. Scowling at the two men, he led Jarrod through a door in the far wall.

The jailhouse took up the front part of the building. It was poorly equipped with just one desk, a battered chair, and a stove on which to boil coffee. The cell area was smaller and had even less in it. It contained only one cell and that had a window but nothing else, not even a bunk, only some dirty straw on the floor.

'In you go, son,' Newley said. He'd never before had an important prisoner in his jail. He didn't know what to do first: go home and tell Mrs Newley or rush down to the saloon and tell Sally, one of the two girls who worked there. They'd both be interested and impressed at his news.

Jarrod sighed heavily as he was pushed inside and the door locked behind him. It looked like he was going to have a long and mighty uncomfortable wait.

EIGHT

Myles Butler walked round the square, taking in the sights and sounds. He tipped his hat to several people, but didn't stop to speak to anyone.

Finally he walked down the short street out near the river, at the end of which was his home.

It still looked how he remembered it. Surrounded by a picket fence, it stood two storeys high, and was made of planks of wood securely nailed together and painted over; glass in the windows. It wasn't large – just one room and a kitchen and, above, two small bedrooms. But it was his.

Home.

Of course, after all these years, it needed repainting; some of the wood would need replacing and the glass in the back bedroom window had a crack across the middle. And the yard was nothing but overgrown weeds. Nothing that couldn't be fixed easily enough.

He pushed open the door and immediately, even before he put his bags down, saw that someone –

Glenda – had been here. As soon as she learnt he was coming home she must have arrived with dustpan and brush and dusters and cleaned and tidied up. And on the kitchen table was a home-baked apple pie.

It made him feel ashamed for the way he'd treated her and he sat down, overwhelmed by it all for a moment. Although he didn't like to admit it, he was somehow disappointed too – he didn't remember it being so small; the walls seemed to be crowding in on him.

Naturally, once word of his arrival spread around town, he found himself the centre of attention, welcomed home by most of the citizens. The party in the room at the back of the general store was lively and noisy, full of good humour. He smiled and shook hands, laughed and joked, and ate the goodies prepared by Glenda and Mrs Ericson.

He had to tell stories about the war, which he only wanted to forget, describe the countryside he'd travelled through, deny having seen President Lincoln, or Robert E. Lee, discuss his plans for the future.

'Well, if you want to start up your carpentry business again, you won't lack for customers,' Ericson told him. 'This is a growing town. A lot of people want houses built, furniture made.'

'What about the land itself? Is any available if I wanted to buy a farm?'

'There's plenty of free land on the other side of

the Sweetwater. Good land too.'

At long last everyone drifted away and Myles was left alone with Glenda.

She put on a shawl to keep out the chill of the evening and, hand in hand, they followed the twisting sandy path that led down through the trees to the Sweetwater River. They came to a halt in a clearing overlooking the water. It was running fast and high between its rocky banks, white-capped waves rippling over the sandy bed, pine trees leaning over the water's edge.

Now they were alone, they suddenly felt awkward with one another and neither could think of anything to say.

At last Glenda managed to find her voice. 'I'm sorry you had to cope with all those people. But it's only natural that they want to hear all about you, especially when they know you're a hero.'

'I did my duty, that's all. And, Glenda,' he paused, adding reluctantly, not wanting to upset or annoy her, 'I must do my duty now.'

'Over Mr Kilkline?'

Butler nodded.

'But why? What is it to do with you?'

'Kilkline killed a Union soldier for no other reason than that the South lost the war. He can't be allowed to get away with it.'

Glenda felt both dismayed, and angry. 'You're not in the army now.'

'I was when it happened.'

'Surely Sheriff Beale can sort it out.'

'I can't wait until he gets here. I don't trust Lester Peabody. He'll do whatever he can to take Kilkline back to Arizona.'

'Then let him.'

'No! It's army business. I've been thinking. I'll pay a visit to Fort Ludlow. See what the commanding officer there has to say. Enlist his help.'

'Oh why?' Glenda cried. 'You've only just got back. We haven't had time or opportunity to be together and now here you are proposing to ride out again.'

'I can't help it. I must go.'

'Oh really!' Glenda took an angry stride away from him and the set look to his mouth, then turned back, eyes sparkling with unshed tears. 'Can't you think of me instead of your precious duty?'

'Please, Glenda, don't be angry with me. Don't let's fight. Please. I won't be gone but a couple of days. Not that long if I can help it. Let me sort this out and then I'll be able to put all my thoughts and energy into what I'm going to do. Don't you think I want that?'

'I don't know. Perhaps once this is done some other piece of duty will crop up that you'll find yourself having to do.'

'No it won't. I want to be with you, sweetheart, very much, but at the moment it just wouldn't be right.'

Glenda could see what whatever she said or did would make no difference. Myles's mind was made up. She couldn't hide the fact that she was disappointed, but she'd waited all this long while for him, she supposed a few more days would make no difference.

Butler reached out for her, pulling her against him. He put his hand under her chin and lifted her face to his. 'And I'm not going to leave until tomorrow morning. We've still got tonight.'

'Oooh,' Sally said, catching hold of Deputy Newley's arm and pulling him close. 'You mean you've got a real-life desperado in your jail?'

'I surely do, ma'am,' Newley preened, taking off his hat and slicking back his hair.

'Ain't you scared?'

' 'Course I ain't. I done told him I won't stand for any nonsense. He's the one scared of me!'

'You're so brave.'

Newley was gratified by Sally's response. Earlier, Mrs Newley had been almost as impressed. If the reaction of the rest of the town was the same perhaps at long last people would take him seriously and not look down their noses at him. Perhaps even Sheriff Beale might have a good word to say about him.

'Can you stay the night?'

'No, no, better get back. Make sure the prisoner is locked up tight. Make sure the town is safe.' Newley left the First Chance Saloon with a more confident step than he'd ever before enjoyed.

The only rooms available, except for those in the First Chance Saloon, were over the general store, breakfast provided by Mrs Ericson. Mr Marsh slept in one, Peabody in the other. Peabody wasn't asleep and not just because he could hear Mr Marsh snoring on the other side of the thin wall.

He still couldn't get his mind round what had happened. Getting out of bed he went over to the window looking out at the thick stand of trees that began just beyond the vegetable garden at the back of the store.

Peabody believed in the law, but he wasn't beyond bending it when it suited him. He could break Jarrod out of the jail (which, given the jail and the deputy, wouldn't be difficult) and would be willing to do so – but then what? There was a lot of empty country out there; Arizona was still a long way away, and he wasn't sure of his bearings.

Peabody recognized Butler's sort. He wouldn't give up easily any more than Peabody would and, in all likelihood, would give chase and, knowing the country, catch up. A jailbreak and flight across the hills would do Peabody's claim to Kilkline no good.

Shivering, he went back to the warmth of the bed, pulling the covers up to his chin. For the moment he didn't know what to do. It was an unusual feeling for him and he didn't like it.

NINE

Peabody liked it even less the following morning when he discovered that Myles Butler had ridden out, at dawn, for Fort Ludlow. There he would receive the support of the army. The army always helped its own.

Fort Ludlow was situated in the middle of a long, narrow valley near to where the foothills petered out into the plains. The spot had been chosen well: close to the hills and plenty of wood, near to the Sweetwater River, while the stagecoach road leading up from Arizona and going on to California was close by. It was also easy to defend with open ground all around.

Not that there was a great deal to defend: no stockade, not even any walls, no gatehouse. Just some one-storey wooden buildings grouped around a parade ground in the centre of which the United States flag fluttered at the top of a tall pole.

There was a corral at the back of the stables, a haybarn, long bunkhouse, one room guardhouse and a row of small shacks making up Officers' Row. The only building of any note was post headquarters, which was two storeys high and had a porch along the front and glass in its windows.

It was late in the afternoon when Butler rode up to the fort. He could see that the troopers had started a vegetable garden in an effort to vary their diet and while the buildings were spartan they were also in good repair.

Some of the men were taking their mounts through their paces in the parade ground. The troopers had clean uniforms and neatly cut hair while the horses were well looked after.

For a moment Butler missed the camaraderie of his army days and wished he hadn't left. Then he remembered the fighting and the dying and the screams of the wounded and wasn't sorry after all.

No one challenged him as he dismounted in front of headquarters, although he was aware that the sergeant shouting out the orders to the mounted troopers was looking over in his direction.

As he stepped up on to the porch, the door opened and a boy came out.

'Freddie!' Butler said in some surprise, as he recognized the boy from the relay station.

'Oh hello, sir.'

'What are you doing here?'

'Just after the stagecoach left some men came by

and robbed us. There were five of 'em.' Remembering what had happened, the boy shuddered. 'One of 'em threatened to shoot Pa. And me.'

Butler put a hand on Freddie's shoulder. It was obvious the boy had been badly frightened. 'Well, he didn't and you shouldn't worry any more.'

'That's what Pa says.'

'He's right.'

'But he thinks they might still be in the area. That's why he sent me here. So Major Sanderson can keep an eye out for 'em.'

'And is he going to?'

'So he says.'

'Then I'm sure the army will catch them.'

'Yes, sir, I hope so.' Freddie didn't look all that convinced by the major's promises or of the army's abilities. 'I'd better be goin', sir. Pa'll be wondering where I am.'

'Perhaps I'll see you around town?'

'Yes, sir. We sometimes come in for supplies.'

Butler felt a bit worried. Would five men, even led by one who sounded trigger-happy, dare try to rob anywhere actually in Sweetwater Crossing? He doubted it. Yet who knew what went on in the minds of outlaws? There were a couple of places, including Ericson's General Store, for which they might believe it was worth taking the risk, as well as making a name for themselves in the process.

He wished he hadn't left Sweetwater so soon after returning home, and now not just because he'd upset Glenda. He had to get back as quickly as he could.

Major Alan Sanderson was in his early forties. He was a tall, spare man with ginger hair, a ginger moustache and green eyes. He'd risen from a lowly second lieutenant to major in the war and, after it was over, led his men out here to establish Fort Ludlow. At the time it had seemed like a good move, but now he often wondered whether it would lead to the hoped for further promotion or whether he would be stuck on the frontier for the rest of his career.

He was strict but fair, liked by his men, and quick to make decisions.

Butler hoped he would now make a decision in his favour.

When he'd finished listening to Butler's story, the major leant back in his chair, lacing his fingers together. 'I agree, Captain, Mr Kilkline killed a Union soldier in Georgia before he committed the robberies in Arizona. Therefore, he is first and foremost the army's prisoner, both by reason of the gravity of the crime and when it took place.'

'Exactly, sir, just as I thought. Mr Peabody won't agree.'

Sanderson frowned. 'He's nothing more than a bounty hunter. He has no authority.'

'He won't agree with that either. And he is ruthless and determined.'

'Can you handle him?'

'Yes, sir. If he plays fair.'

'You don't think he will?'

'As you said, sir, he's a bounty hunter and he doesn't have to follow any rules except his own.'

'Umm, I see.' The major stood up and went over to the window looking out at the parade ground. 'What do you want me to do?'

'Have you got some men who can come back to Sweetwater Crossing with me? They can take Kilkline into custody and bring him back here. Peabody won't be able to argue with them or you.'

A number of army men would also deter the robbers from coming to the town.

'Unfortunately, Sergeant Cook is out with a troop chasing after some hostiles making a nuisance of themselves and I need my other sergeant here.'

Butler had the feeling Sanderson wasn't taking it all that seriously; but then the major didn't know Lester Peabody. 'I'd appreciate it if you could help me.'

'I suppose I could let you have a couple of troopers. . . .'

Two men, Butler thought, realizing from the look on Sanderson's face that he would have to be satisfied. He just hoped they would be enough.

'Major, what about the gang of robbers in the area?'

'You know about them?'

'I saw the boy from the stagecoach station.'

'Ah yes, Freddie. A good lad. From what he says

they sound a bad bunch. Normally, of course, the army isn't responsible for catching thieves.'

'Surely out here where the law is a long way away, exceptions can be made?'

'Naturally they can. That's why I told the boy I'd see what I could do and also why I've sent a rider after Sergeant Cook ordering him to look out for this gang at the same time as searching for the hostiles. It's all I can do. Now, Captain,' – Butler realized he was about to be dismissed – 'you can leave in the morning.'

'The morning? Not now?'

'No, Captain, not now. You won't get far before it gets dark. And this country is too dangerous to travel at night. Why take risks for the sake of a few hours?'

Butler supposed the man was right.

'Speak to my orderly. He'll arrange for somewhere for you to sleep.'

'Thank you, sir.'

TEN

Jarrod got up from the floor and went over to the tiny window, not that there was anything or anyone for him to see. The cell looked out on to an alley running along the back of the buildings which was hardly ever used.

He felt both tired and dirty. Time was dragging with no one to talk to and nothing to see or do – except worry about his future.

For most of the afternoon the sun had shone in through the window, making the cell hot and stuffy, but during the night it had been so cold he'd curled up amongst the straw unable to sleep. The food Deputy Newley had brought him had been practically uneatable, the coffee strong and bitter and Newley hadn't bothered to give his prisoner a blanket. Nor had he stopped to tell him what was happening. It was as if he was scared of his prisoner and wanted as little to do with him as possible.

Of Lester Peabody – or Myles Butler – Jarrod had seen no sign.

Yawning, stretching wearily, Jarrod was about to turn away and sit down again when movement in the alley caught his eye.

Five riders heading for the back of the livery stable.

Two of the men were, despite the difference in their ages, obviously brothers. Another had a vacant look on his face and one was only about twenty and was looking round with an air of expectancy.

And bringing up the rear. . . .

Jesus Christ!

Jarrod took a quick step away from the window, his heart hammering wildly, sweat breaking out on the palms of his hands.

Harry Phillips!

It couldn't be.

He risked another glance out of the window.

It was! Harry Phillips – here in Sweetwater Crossing! It wasn't possible, yet there he was, as large as life and looking wilder than ever.

What was he doing here? Was Phillips following him? Still after him for, as Harry would see it, turning traitor? Surely he couldn't be. How could he have followed the trail all this way?

Yet if not, what was he here for? And with four other men. Up to no good, that was for sure. Jarrod might be a reluctant outlaw, but he was enough of a one to recognize his own wary stance in others.

He swung round as the door from the office opened.

'Didn't want your grub?' Newley bent down to pick up the tray of almost untouched food. 'Can't say I rightly blame you none. Mrs Newley ain't much of a cook. . . . What's up? You look like you've seen a ghost.'

'Close enough.' Jarrod went up to the cell door, grasping the bars. 'Look, can you get Mr Peabody to come see me?'

'What for?'

'It's important.'

'I said what for?'

'I need to tell him something.'

'What?'

Jarrod sighed. It was obvious Newley was filled with his own importance having a wanted outlaw in his jailhouse, determined to show everyone, including his prisoner, that he was in charge.

'I just seen someone. A man I knew in Arizona. . . .'

'Another stagecoach robber?' Newley leered at him.

'Yeah,' Jarrod admitted. 'Peabody will want to know. He needs to know.'

'Yeah, well, son, I know now, don't I?' Newley turned away.

'What are you going to do?'

'I'll handle it; don't you worry none.'

'You will tell Peabody, won't you?'

Newley glanced back. 'That's for me to know and you to guess at.'

Goddammit, he didn't believe Jarrod, must have thought it was some sort of deception.

'Tell him it's Harry Phillips!' Jarrod yelled in despair.

'Sure thing, son.' And with a laugh Newley shut the door.

Jarrod sank down on the straw, back to the wall. Newley was a goddamned idiot. He wasn't going to do anything. Peabody would be furious when he found out.

And Harry Phillips would be left free and clear to do whatever he'd come to Sweetwater Crossing for.

'So this is Sweetwater Crossing?' Harry Phillips said, swinging easily down from his horse.

'Yeah.' Wincott beckoned him to the double doors leading from the stable onto the street. 'And over there is the general store.'

'We ain't gonna rob it till tomorrow, are we?' Melvin said anxiously from by their side. 'We are goin' over to the saloon tonight, ain't we?'

Actually, Wincott would have liked to commit the robbery and get out of town as quickly as possible; to hang around would mean that later on some of the townspeople would be able to identify them. But the others needed a drink, the chance to relax – Christ, he needed the same – and Melvin was anxious to visit a whore.

So he nodded. 'Yeah we'll go over there after we've seen to the horses and had something to eat.

That OK with you, Harry?'

Much to Wincott's surprise and relief, Phillips made no objection to the plan, but simply nodded his agreement.

Lester Peabody stepped outside of the store. It was early evening and he'd just finished his supper, during which he'd been forced to listen to Mr Marsh extolling the virtues of his sale goods. He was heartily fed up with the enforced inactivity of the day. He wasn't used to it. Didn't like it. Wasn't going to put up with it much longer.

He'd seen Glenda Gardiner from time to time during the day. It was obvious she'd been crying and over supper she was still near to tears. Of course, he would have put duty before the pleasures of being reunited with a girl, but he was both surprised and annoyed Butler had done the same.

He was also surprised when Deputy Newley made it plain he wasn't letting Peabody – or anyone else – near the prisoner until Captain Butler got back from the fort. If he wasn't willing to be more accommodating, Deputy Newley would find himself in line for an unpleasant confrontation.

Rather than sit, fretting, alone in his room, Lester decided to while away the evening in the First Chance Saloon.

The saloon had few pretensions. The bar ran along the rear of the square room and consisted of some planks on empty barrels. A few tables and chairs stood in the middle of the room. It was lit by smelly oil lamps and provided with plenty of spittoons. In case anyone missed them there was straw on the floor. A staircase at one side led upstairs to where the whores entertained their customers.

The place didn't employ many girls, just two in fact. One was a plump blonde with a loud laugh. She was hanging on the arm of Mr Marsh, who had got here before him. The other was a redheaded girl who, if not exactly pretty, was well set up with a low-cut dress showing off her figure.

This early the saloon was nearly empty. Apart from Mr Marsh, the only other customers were a couple of very young cowboys, who acted as if they were being very daring drinking in a saloon. Peabody was able to get a seat in the corner where he could watch all that went on and protect his back at the same time.

He had almost finished his beer when the redheaded girl sauntered over to him, carrying another drink.

'My name's Sally. Yours is Lester, ain't it?'

News obviously travelled fast in such a small town.

'Mind if I sit down?'

'No.' Peabody indicated the seat opposite him. Up close, he could see she was older than she first appeared with little wrinkles at the corners of her eyes. But those eyes still had a twinkle in them.

'Anything I can do for you, sugar?' Sally leant further across the table showing off more of her bosom.

Oh well, why not? It had been a long time since Peabody had had a girl, redheaded or not.

He stood up and held out his hand to her.

No sooner had Peabody gone upstairs with Sally than Harry Phillips, at the head of the gang, pushed his way in through the doors. Not that Peabody would have recognized him. Although the man had been described to Peabody, his appearance had changed dramatically from when he'd been robbing stagecoaches in Griffin Creek. But Peabody would have recognized the type and, unlike Deputy Newley, perhaps done something about the five men.

'Five beers and a bottle of your best whiskey,' Phillips yelled out to the bartender. 'None of the watered-down stuff.' He went over to a table and sat down, staring moodily around. 'Christ, what a dump. Come on, goddammit, where are those drinks! We're thirsty!'

The one remaining girl in the saloon reluctantly carried them over to the table. She, too, could recognize trouble when she saw it.

She needn't have worried; one glance at her and Phillips dismissed her as too old. He hadn't had a woman in ages, but he wasn't desperate enough to take just anyone. She might do for Melvin though; he'd obviously need someone with experience because for sure he wouldn't know what to do otherwise.

'There ain't even a game of cards goin' on.'

'Mebbe there will be later,' Wincott said.

'Yeah, and I don't suppose none of these hicks'll have much to bet.'

'Well,' Wincott said impatiently, 'if they're such hicks you won't have much trouble in winning every hand, will you?'

Phillips laughed. 'Iffen I do, I'll cheat.'

The trouble was, Wincott thought, he wasn't joking. Phillips had told them all about the duels he'd fought over cheating at cards; although who was cheating and whether the duels took place only in his imagination, Wincott was never sure.

Glenda lay alone and awake in her room, wondering where Myles was – whether he had reached the fort safely and was perhaps on his way back to her. She was worried and scared. Although he'd tried to hide it she'd seen the look in his eyes when he thought no one was watching. Despite Sweetwater Crossing figuring in his hopes and dreams throughout the war, now he was home the reality somehow hadn't lived up to those hopes.

She turned over yet again, pulling the blankets around her, trying to get warm. What would he do? Would he be content to remain here? And if not, if he left, where would he go and would he want to take her with him?

There was certainly something about redheaded girls. Peabody couldn't remember having had such a good time in a long while and because Peabody was as good a lover as he was fighter, nor could Sally. Now they lay, curled up in one another's arms, under the warm blankets on the bed.

'You're a bounty hunter, ain't you?' Sally traced a hand down Peabody's slim chest.

'I don't particularly like the description but, yes, I suppose that's what I could be called.'

Sally giggled. 'You talk real strange. Why?'

'Why do I talk strange?'

'No, silly. Why are you a bounty hunter?'

Peabody thought about that. Why, exactly, had he become what he had? He supposed part of the answer lay in his childhood.

'If I'd stayed in the East where I grew up I guess I'd have become a farmer or maybe a clerk in a store or an office. That was the limit of my folks' ambition for me and my brothers.'

'And you didn't want that?'

Peabody shook his head. 'Where's the excitement in handling a plough or writing with a pen?'

'So you're doing it for excitement?'

'Partly,' Peabody admitted. 'I also believe I'm doing the country a service by ridding it of outlaws who prey on innocent people.'

'There you go with all them big words again!'

'Sorry.'

'Can you remember the first man you caught?'

'Yes. He'd robbed my uncle, shot him too. I went after him. Got my uncle's money back, made sure he couldn't shoot anyone else. Collected a reward.

Made up my mind what to do with my life.'

Sally thought there had to be more to it than that – especially for him to have become so good at what he did – but that Peabody probably didn't fully understand himself why he'd become what he had.

'Do you like what you do?'

Peabody thought about that as well. 'I'm not sure *like* is the right word. I am extremely good at it. No outlaw I've been after has ever escaped me. And except where the man himself has made it impossible for me to do so I've brought them all in alive.'

'Have you ever regretted bringing anyone in?'

'No. All those I've gone after have deserved to be locked up or hanged.'

'Haven't you ever thought that maybe someone didn't have any choice but to take to robbery?'

Peabody had never, not even from the earliest days of his 'bounty hunting', let his heart rule his head. 'Everyone has a choice. I don't believe all this business of being forced into doing something through unforeseen circumstances.'

'Sometimes we have to do things we don't want to.' Sally was thinking of herself. She'd have preferred to be a wife and mother rather than a prostitute in a saloon but her life hadn't worked out that way.

'It's not my problem. If there's a Wanted poster out on someone and I'm hired to bring him in, then that's what I'll do. The rights or wrongs of it don't concern me. It's up to a jury to decide whether the prisoner is guilty or not and the judge to take into consideration the whys and wherefores before he passes sentence.'

Sally sat up, hugging her arms across her breasts. 'What about the young man you've got in the jail? Deputy Newley says he's dangerous.' Despite what Newley thought, Sally didn't always believe all he told her.

'Jarrod Kilkline.' Peabody paused thoughtfully. 'No, he's not dangerous. In fact I guess he's pretty harmless and I'm sure he's sorry for what he did. But, what the hell, he did do wrong and however sorry he is now he should be made to pay for it.'

'It seems a bit harsh to me.'

'Maybe it is. But it's my way. My code. I can't change it. I don't want to.' Peabody reached up to stroke her hair. 'Let's stop being so serious. I don't often have the chance to be with a pretty lady like you. Come here.'

Sally slid back down by him. 'Stay the night.'

He could see nothing wrong with that idea.

Harry Phillips drank steadily from the bottle of whiskey. The drink didn't seem to affect him, except to make him more foul-tempered, especially when no card games started up and no pretty whores came into the saloon. His mood affected the others, making them jumpy and irritable. The only one to enjoy himself was Melvin, who went off with the blonde whore and came back with a huge smile on his face.

When it got near midnight, Wincott said, 'We'd better go.'

'Why the hell?'

'Because we wanna be up early tomorrow. . . .'

'Oh yeah, so we can make a lot of money robbing the general store.'

'Hush!' Wincott glanced up. No one had heard, because the saloon was empty except for the bartender who, although keeping a wary, worried eye on them, wasn't near enough to hear what they said.

'Big deal!' Mumbling and swearing, Phillips got up, kicking the chair away from under him. 'We won't get much from that. And tonight we've gotta sleep in the livery stable. Hell!'

Behind them, the bartender quickly locked up in case they changed their minds and came back.

Deputy Newley lay awake beside his snoring wife, wishing he could be with Sally. Was there anything in what that Jarrod Kilkline fellow had said? He'd seemed worried. Should he have done anything about it? No . . . no. Kilkline was lying for some reason of his own. Trying to make Newley look like a fool. Well he wasn't going to fall for that!

Satisfied, Newley turned over and, mind full of thoughts of Sally, fell asleep at last.

Jarrod was also lying awake and not just because it was cold and hard on the cell floor.

Peabody hadn't put in an appearance; that fool,

Newley, couldn't have passed the message on. Perhaps, with luck, Phillips was just passing through but Jarrod doubted it. There had been something furtive about the group of men.

That wasn't the only thing on Jarrod's mind: he'd escaped the clutches of the law before – he couldn't see himself doing so this time and after a day and two nights in this cell he was already going crazy. How would he cope with a long jail sentence? It would be better to face the hangman.

It wasn't fair; he hadn't asked for any of this. It was the fault of the Union Army. Jarrod rolled over on his other side and gave himself up to a fit of self-pity.

ELEVEN

Myles Butler was up early, anxious to be on his way back to Sweetwater Crossing. He'd hardly slept for worrying about what might be happening in the town and frustration at being unable to do anything about it. He was saddling his horse when two troopers came into the stables behind him.

'Privates Campbell and Thomas,' the one called Campbell announced. 'We've been detailed to go to Sweetwater Crossing with you, pick up a prisoner.'

Butler eyed them in some disappointment. They were both very young, little more than twenty or twenty-one. They might be capable of handling Jarrod Kilkline, but would they be able to handle Lester Peabody? Should he ask Major Sanderson for men with more experience? The major might listen to him, but did he really want to spend more precious time here? No, these two would have to do.

'I want to be on my way as soon as I've saddled up.'

'Don't worry, sir,' Thomas said cheerfully. 'We won't delay you. We're ready to go.'

It was later than normal the next morning when Peabody woke up. Sally was still asleep and he slipped out of bed, washed and dressed without her stirring. He kissed her cheek and, smiling in memory of their night together, went out of the room, down the stairs and out of the saloon.

There in the road he stood and stretched. It was a lovely morning. Quite warm already, no breeze and just a few clouds in the sky to the west.

When he got back to the store, Glenda was helping Mrs Ericson tidy the shelves, and Ericson was discussing with Mr Marsh whether or not to buy some of the articles the drummer had for sale. No one said anything about where Peabody might have spent the night, although they probably all guessed. Mrs Ericson certainly looked a bit disapproving.

'Oh dear, you've missed breakfast,' she said, in a tone that told him it served him right.

'Would you like me to cook you something?' Glenda asked.

Peabody shook his head. 'No, I 'm not hungry.'

No one had the chance to do or say any more.

The door was suddenly banged open. Five men rushed in. They all had their guns drawn and the one with long hair and buckskins, yelled, 'Hands up, all of you, don't try nothin' goddamned foolish! You're being robbed!' He sounded excited.

Mrs Ericson gave a startled cry and dropped the bale of cloth she held. Immediately, Glenda put her arms round the woman drawing her out of the way. Ericson and Mr Marsh stopped what they were doing to gape.

Peabody quickly stepped backwards into as much shadow as a pile of stacked furs allowed him. Even if these men didn't work out that he was on the side of the law, they would nevertheless see he was different to the others and, therefore, a target.

Phillips strode over to the counter, kicking a barrel of nails out of the way and scattering tins and bottles off the counter. Glass shattered, tins fell everywhere and nails rolled about on the floor.

'There ain't no real need for that,' Wincott objected, as Mrs Ericson cried out again.

Phillips took no notice. Nonchalantly, he put an elbow on the counter and leaned across it waving his gun in Ericson's face. 'Hand over your money. All of it. And hurry it up.'

The two Wincott brothers kept an eye on the others while Melvin Stack and Tom Ryan wandered around examining the goods they thought worth stealing.

'There's plenty of food here,' Melvin said.

'Then pack it up,' Wincott said. 'Use a gunny sack to put it in.'

'OK. C'mon, Tom, help me.'

Peabody was not pleased. It didn't sit well with him that he was in the store while it was being robbed and he could do nothing about it. He glanced across at Mr Marsh who shook his head slightly. Mr Marsh might have helped him, but he was stopped by the same thing as Peabody: there were two women present – and three children in the back room who might come in at any moment.

'All right, all right,' Ericson said, a sheen of sweat breaking out on his forehead. 'Take it easy. I'll give you what you want.'

'Just see you do.' Still waving his gun about, Phillips followed the man as he went over to the till, which was near to where Mrs Ericson and Glenda stood, arms around each other. He tipped his hat to them. 'Good morning, ma'am, pretty miss, we won't be here long, so long as you all behave yourselves.'

'Don't keep threatening them,' Wincott said angrily. 'They're doing what we want.'

But it was obvious to Peabody that the man liked threatening those over whom he held power.

With shaking hands, Ericson opened the till and gathered up the money. 'Here you are, mister.' He handed it over. 'Take it and go.'

Phillips looked at the money. A look of disgust came over his face. 'Where's the goddamned rest of it?'

'That's all there is, mister, please, I'm telling the truth.'

'No, you ain't. You're cheating us!' Phillips's voice rose to an ugly yell.

'C'mon, Harry,' Wincott urged. 'Let's go.'

'Not till we get it all.'

'There's nothing more.' Mrs Ericson added her own plea to her husband's.

'You lying bitch!' Phillips turned to Wincott. 'Hell, these goddamned hicks are holding out on us and you're goddamned letting 'em. Well, the bastards ain't gonna get the better of me!' Spittle flew from Phillips's lips as he worked himself up into a fine fury.

'Look, take my money too.' Mr Marsh held out his wallet.

'I don't want your goddamn money. I want his!' Phillips flung the notes and coins he held down on the floor. 'Stupid, lying sonofabitch,' he said, and shot Ericson.

The gunfire echoed with the screams of Mrs Ericson and Glenda and the cry of Ericson as he grabbed at his chest and staggered backwards.

Peabody knew the man was dead before he hit the floor.

'Jesus Christ! Harry!' Wincott cried. 'What the hell did you do that for?'

'I felt like it,' Phillips said with a grin. 'Feel like shooting a few other people too.' And he turned the gun towards Mrs Ericson.

At the sound of the shot, Jarrod leapt to his feet. He went over to the cell's window, angry and scared because he couldn't see anything. What was happening? It had to be something Harry Phillips was up to! It had to be.

In the office, Deputy Newley didn't know what to do. He didn't want to do anything, but if he was to be re-elected he had to at least show willing. At this time of the morning the shot couldn't mean much, could it? It surely had nothing to do with what Kilkline had said.

Yet perhaps it could because suddenly the air was filled with a great many more shots.

In the store mayhem broke out.

Glenda shoved Mrs Ericson away and down, throwing herself on top of the woman.

Nearest to Phillips, Curtis Wincott grappled with the man, trying to get hold of his gun.

Mr Marsh dived behind the counter, pulling out his gun, while Ryan and Stack, the one simple, the other young, and both worked up, began firing their guns; not that they were really shooting at anyone they were simply letting off steam.

'Now see what the hell you've done!' Wincott yelled angrily at Phillips. 'Let's get outa here!' He began to back towards the door, swinging his gun this way and that, unwilling to fire it, while Curtis pulled Phillips after him.

One of Peabody's hidden guns suddenly appeared in his hand. He stepped out from the shadows, aimed and fired. The bullet narrowly missed Phillips ploughing into the wall by his head.

Both Ryan and Melvin turned in Peabody's direction and shot at him. Peabody shot back. They missed. He didn't. One bullet struck Melvin high in the shoulder and a second one in his side.

The young man gave a screech of pain and surprise and staggered against Ryan, who caught hold of him.

Wincott had the door open and he, Curtis and Phillips were already out on the sidewalk. Ryan dragged Melvin after him and Wincott kicked the door shut. They all dashed to the horses left outside the store and together Wincott and Ryan got Melvin up into the saddle.

Phillips, laughing and yelling, looked around him, ready and hoping for more trouble. He found it when he caught a glimpse of movement over by the jailhouse and the wink of a deputy's star. 'Aw hell!' he said, as the lawman came into view and sent several shots in that direction.

Newley was picked up off his feet and slammed down with the force of the bullets striking his body. Blood seeped out into the dusty ground around him.

'Let's go!' Wincott yelled. He dug heels into the sides of his horse, the others did likewise and, heads down, they galloped out of town.

TWELVE

By the time Peabody reached the door he was too late: Deputy Newley was dead and the gang had all but disappeared, leaving behind nothing but a dust cloud.

Men and women began to rush from the buildings to find out what had happened. There were demands and screams. Some paused by their deputy while others crowded round outside the store, some going inside.

Sally came out of the saloon and saw Mrs Newley crouched down by the deputy. She went to her immediately and the two women put aside their jealousies over the same man and cried together.

Peabody turned back into the store. The only sound now – loud in the sudden quiet as everyone fell silent trying to take in the scene – was that of Mrs Ericson weeping over the body of her dead husband, while Glenda tried to comfort her. The three children had come in and stood in a huddle, unable to understand what had happened. Mr Marsh stared helplessly at him.

'Get Mrs Ericson upstairs,' Peabody said. 'She can't do any good here. Take the kids too. And someone had better go for the undertaker. You do have an undertaker, I suppose?'

'Old Bart, the livery owner buries people,' someone said.

'Then fetch him.'

No one questioned Peabody's right to take charge. This sort of thing rarely happened in Sweetwater Crossing and recognizing experienced authority when they saw it, there seemed no reason not to follow his orders.

'The bastards,' Mr Marsh said. 'That 'un shot Ericson for no good reason.'

'Except his own enjoyment.'

'What happens now?'

Peabody shrugged and didn't reply.

In a clearing amongst the trees, high above the town, Wincott drew the others to a halt. He could never remember being so furious or so frightened. Even worse, as Phillips dismounted and took a drink from his canteen, it seemed he wasn't sorry or even worried; if anything he looked pleased with himself.

Ryan lifted Melvin, who was grey-faced with pain, from the horse and laid the boy on the ground. 'You'll be OK, boy, hear me?'

'It hurts, Tom, oh, it hurts.'

'Hang on, we'll get you help.'

Wincott, closely followed by Curtis, strode over to Phillips. 'What the hell was all that about?' he yelled, catching hold of the man's shoulder, swinging him round, dropping his hand as he saw the glint in Phillips's eyes. 'Not only ain't we got any money from the store . . .'

'There weren't much anyway. That was the trouble. That sonofabitch was holding out on us.'

'No, he wasn't. He gave you everything he had.' Wincott took a deep, steadying breath. 'Now, like I said, we ain't got any money and two men are dead, one a deputy in case you hadn't noticed, and for no good reason than that you lost your temper.'

Phillips shrugged, unconcerned.

'What's the matter with you, are you mad?' But that was just it, Wincott thought, Phillips was mad. There could be no other explanation for his behaviour.

'And Melvin is shot,' Curtis added. 'Badly too. The poor kid is hurting.'

'Oh, well, if that's a problem I can soon put it right.' Phillips pushed by the two brothers and went over to where Ryan was wiping ineffectually at the blood seeping out of Melvin's side.

'What are you doin'?' Curtis demanded in some panic.

'I'm goin' to shoot him, put him out of his misery.'

'For God's sake!' Wincott protested.

Ryan looked up, startled, fear and fury appearing

in his eyes. 'Touch him and you die!'

Phillips flung up his arms in ill-natured surrender. 'All right, all right, it was a joke. Christ, ain't any of you got a sense of humour?'

'Unfortunately, Harry, I can't see anything funny in this situation. It could have been any one of us – or all of us – who got shot.'

'Well, we didn't, so what the hell are you complaining about? Who was that bastard in there anyhow? Good shot whoever he was, cool under pressure.' Phillips sounded admiring.

'That hardly matters.'

'What we goin' to do?' Ryan asked. 'Melvin needs a doctor.'

'I don't think there is a doctor round here,' Curtis pointed out. 'And we can't go back to town.'

'He needs someone to look after him,' Ryan said. Adding quickly, 'We ain't leaving him.' In case Phillips suggested such a thing.

He didn't, saying instead, 'We need to get outa here.'

'Yeah, thanks to you,' Curtis said.

'Don't keep on about it.'

'Shut up!' Wincott shouted, quietening them all. 'Let's stop this arguing amongst ourselves. What's done is done.' He wasn't best pleased about it, but this was neither the time nor the place to settle with Harry; that could come later when they were all safe. 'Like Tom says, we need to get help for Melvin and we have to get away. Even a place like Sweetwater

Crossing will be able to put out a posse. And with a deputy dead we'll have all sorts of lawmen after us, too.'

'Where are we goin' to go?' Curtis asked. 'What about back to the stagecoach station?'

Wincott shook his head. 'It's too far. And the posse might think we'll try to escape by getting on a stagecoach. Anyway, thanks to Harry, the owner, if he sees us comin', won't take any chances, but will shoot first and see what we want later. No, we'll ride up into the hills. There must be some place there, a farm, small ranch, something, where we can find shelter.'

'OK, so let's get goin',' Phillips said, going over to his horse. 'I can't see what all the fuss and bother is about.'

Sweetwater Crossing was in an angry turmoil: two men killed – one a deputy, the other a good family man. Two widows, one left with three young children.

Other men gathered outside the general store, deciding to form a posse and go after those responsible. They were willing and eager but inexperienced, no leader or tracker amongst them. No one knew what to do.

Old Bart had been and gone and the two bodies were now lying at the livery stable.

Slowly, Glenda came down from the bedroom where Mrs Ericson was sitting with her three children. She could do nothing for them but let them cry together, as they tried to understand that husband and father was dead. Lester Peabody stood in the store doorway watching the activities outside.

Going up to him, she said, 'You will help, won't you? Head the posse? Show them what to do?'

Peabody shook his head. 'This is nothing to do with me.'

'But you're the only one who can do it! Why won't you? Oh, I see,' she added bitterly, 'you're still intent on leaving with Jarrod Kilkline, aren't you? That's all that matters to you.'

Peabody didn't reply, although that was his intention. It seemed the ideal opportunity to slip away with Kilkline while everyone's attention was on the gang of killers and no one would bother about them.

'How could you?' Glenda's eyes glittered angrily. 'Don't you care that two men have been killed? That a woman has been left with three fatherless children?'

'Of course I care.'

'But not enough to do anything? Because you care more about your pride?'

'Miss Gardiner, Captain Butler will soon be back in town, the army is nearby. They'll be quite capable of chasing a gang that didn't seem to be endowed with too many brains.'

'By then the gang will have a good head start.'

'Not that much of a one. Someone should go and fetch Sheriff Beale.'

'We don't know where he is.'

'Well, I'm sorry, but I'm not going to argue any more.'

Firmly telling himself he was right and to take no notice of Glenda's anger or his own inner urgings to go after the men responsible for all this, Peabody packed his possessions in his saddle-bags and left the store. He kept to the alleyways, taking the long way round to the jail, not wanting to get involved with those still milling around in the square. In the jail-house, he found the key to the cell.

'What's happened?' Jarrod demanded. 'What's going on?'

'The store was robbed, two men including Newley, are dead.'

With Phillips involved, Jarrod wasn't surprised. 'What are you doing?' he asked, as Peabody went to unlock the cell door.

'We're leaving.'

'Ain't you going after the killers?'

'No, why should I?'

'Because,' Jarrod said, 'Harry Phillips was a member of the gang and I just bet he was the one pulled the trigger!'

THIRTEEN

'What!' Peabody took a step backwards in shock. Then his face turned hard. 'You're lying.'

'No, I ain't.'

'You only want me to go after them so you can escape again.'

'Maybe I do, but that don't change the fact that Harry was here. Tall, long hair, a scar down the side of his face? I'm right, ain't I? I told Newley I wanted to see you; I guess he didn't bother to say anything.'

'No.'

'If he had he might be alive now.'

'Are you telling me the truth?'

'Yeah.'

'You'd better be.' Peabody thought he was. He remembered one of the others calling the shooter 'Harry'. 'I guess I'll be heading up that posse after all.'

'What about me? Butler will be back any time now. Without you around there'll be nothing to stop him from handing me over to the army.'

Peabody's eyes narrowed. That was true. And he didn't like it.

'Unfortunately, I don't think the good people of Sweetwater Crossing will take kindly to having a wanted outlaw joining their manhunt. No, you stay here. If necessary I can take up your capture with the army later on.'

He had no intention of meekly handing Jarrod over to the army. On the other hand, Phillips was the one he wanted most of all; and not just because of his part in the stagecoach robberies down in Arizona, more particularly because he'd also held up Peabody at the point of a gun. Peabody had been in the same room as Harry Phillips and the man had got away. The fact that it was no fault of his made it no easier for Lester to stomach.

'Be careful,' Jarrod said.

When Peabody reappeared at the store, Glenda looked up from where she was trying to sweep away the mess Phillips had left behind.

'Forgotten something?' she asked sarcastically.

'I've changed my mind.'

'Why?'

'There's no time to explain.'

If Glenda wondered why the man was now in such a hurry to go after a gang he'd earlier dismissed as too stupid to escape, she, too, felt an explanation could come later. The important thing was to catch them.

'Look, Miss Gardiner, you seem about the most sensible person in town. . . .'

Glenda wasn't sure whether to be flattered or not.

'When Captain Butler gets back send him after us. I'd like someone experienced at pulling a trigger with me.'

Peabody had seen the four or five men who'd finally decided to form the posse, Mr Marsh being one of them. While they were probably familiar with guns they didn't look like the type he wanted at his back going up against someone like Harry Phillips.

'And perhaps you can see that Mr Kilkline gets something to eat and drink?'

It was quickly obvious to Myles Butler that something was wrong. No one was about on the streets. The stores were closed. Even the saloon doors were shut.

With Campbell and Thomas close behind him he galloped up to the store and leapt from his horse.

'Do you want us to come in with you?'

'No, you stay here.' Fearing the worst and wanting to be alone to face it, Butler rushed into the store.

Whatever had happened, part of it had happened in here – there was glass swept up into a corner, a barrel lying on its side, blood seeping into the wooden planks of the floor.

Heart thumping with fear he called out, 'Glenda!' Oh please, please, he thought, let her be all right. 'Glenda, sweetheart, where are you?'

At the sound of his voice, Glenda ran down the

stairs and crying, as she hadn't yet done, threw herself into his arms.

'What is it?'

'Oh, Myles, it's been dreadful,' she sobbed. 'Thank God you're here.'

Not long afterwards, Butler, grim faced and purposeful, left the store. It was stupid to blame himself for what had happened. He couldn't have known, couldn't have done anything against five men even if he had been present; all the same, he did do so. Duty had come first and now two men were dead and Glenda had had to face men with guns. He'd find it hard to forgive himself.

The two troopers had ridden down to the jail-house and were standing outside Jarrod's cell. Butler quickly told them about the robbery.

'You two can take Kilkline back to Fort Ludlow on your own, can't you?'

'Of course we can, Cap'n,' Campbell said. 'If we start out in the morning we'll be there by early evening. We can also tell Major Sanderson about what's happened here. What will you be doing?'

'Going after the posse.'

'Don't worry 'bout us,' Thomas added. 'You catch up with those bastards. Go on.' As Butler hurried back outside, Thomas turned to Jarrod. 'You ain't thinking 'bout giving us any trouble I hope.'

Handcuffed, weaponless, with two young but disciplined troopers in attendance, Jarrod didn't see how he was supposed to cause trouble. He wasn't happy at the thought of being handed over to the army, but he couldn't do anything about that either.

'Promise me you'll be careful,' Glenda begged as she watched Butler pack up the few things he needed for the trail.

'You needn't ask me that.' Butler turned to her, taking her in his arms. 'I'm so sorry about it all.'

'It wasn't your fault; it wasn't anyone's fault.'

'Will you be all right here on your own?'

'Yes.'

'I love you.'

A few minutes later, Glenda stood on the sidewalk watching after Butler as he rode away. With a shiver she turned back inside the store. She had seen the look in that man's eyes as he'd pulled the trigger and killed Mr Ericson. He'd done it casually, with no more concern than if he'd been shooting down a rabid animal. Myles had survived the long years of the war, she couldn't bear to lose him now. Yet she also knew there was no way she could have asked him not to go.

It was dark by the time Butler caught up with the posse. Lester Peabody had left an easy trail for him to follow through the trees and rocks, up into the hills. Knowing it was useless to track the gang at night, the man had called a halt. A fire was lit, coffee on the boil, bacon frying.

As he approached, thinking the posse might well be itchy and not wanting to risk getting shot, Butler called out his name. Told to come on in, he rode into the circle of the fire and, dismounting, went over to where Peabody sat by the fire, hunkering down by him.

'How's it going?'

'Not too good.' Peabody sounded unwilling to admit that the gang might be getting the better of him. 'They know what they're doing, or at least Phillips does.'

'Who's Phillips?'

'Kilkline's friend from Arizona.'

'Oh yes, I remember you mentioning him. He's here?'

'Evidently. He's a real bastard. He was in the CSA too where he must have learnt things like hiding his tracks. The fact they've got a wounded man with them doesn't seem to be slowing them down. Where do you think they'll head?'

Butler shrugged. 'It depends on how well they know the area. Iffen I was them I'd keep to the hills for as long as I could then make for the desert where I could ride hell bent for leather for the border. They might have different plans. I guess all we can do is follow 'em.'

Peabody nodded in agreement, although he didn't like it. He liked to be as much ahead of the game as possible. In the circumstances there was no choice.

Harry Phillips strode around the small clearing

where, eventually, they'd stopped for the night. He was still too worked up for sleep. And he was now in charge, the troop commander, for none of the others had the know-how to lose the enemy who had started after them. He was the one to make plans, the one to say which way they should ride, when to stop, the one to refuse to let them have a fire, even when Melvin was shivering from loss of blood.

Listening to Melvin groaning in his sleep, he allowed himself to feel sorry for Private Stack. But in every engagement you risked casualties. It couldn't be helped.

And it had been exciting. Everyone scared of him. Yells of fright and pain. Bullets flying around.

Just like the old days.

FOURTEEN

They'd set out early in the morning.

The two troopers ignored Jarrod. He rode slightly ahead of them so they could keep a careful eye on him. If Jarrod harboured hopes that maybe, somewhere and somehow, he could escape them, those hopes were quickly dashed.

The fact the two soldiers had spent most of the night in the saloon, which had reopened on the understanding that the town's mourners would want somewhere to drown their sorrows, didn't impair their efficiency. They made it plain they wouldn't stand any nonsense.

And now they were almost halfway to Fort Ludlow, travelling along a narrow shelf of land that crossed the side of a steep hill, trees crouching close on both sides of the track.

'We'd better stop for a while,' Thomas said, looking up at the hot noon sun. 'Give the horses a rest.'

Jarrod slid awkwardly off his horse's back and

accepted a canteen of water from Campbell. 'How much longer?'

'Four hours mebbe,' Campbell said, before his eyes widened in sudden startled surprise.

'What is it?' Jarrod said, wondering what was wrong.

At the same time Campbell's chest seemed to explode and Jarrod was sprayed with the man's blood.

Jarrod cried out in shock and took a quick step backwards, stumbling, even as Campbell also fell to the ground. A few seconds later came the sound of a rifleshot from somewhere on the slope of the hill.

Thomas swung round to see what was happening. 'Hell!' he exclaimed, and went to pull out his gun. He didn't even get it out of the holster before he, too, was shot.

Heart thumping, wondering what on earth was going on – was it Indians up there on the slope? Thomas had spoken to Campbell about hostiles in the area – sure he, too, was about to be killed, Jarrod lay on the ground. His eyes searched the hills, looking for the shooter, seeing nothing and no one. Keeping low he squirmed backwards towards the horses. There were no more shots, but was that because he was out of the killer's line of sight or for some other reason?

He knew it was the latter when he heard not an Indian's cry but a Rebel yell.

Oh God, it was Harry Phillips! It had to be.

And now he saw movement amongst the trees. Men on horseback coming down towards him.

He had to get away. He jumped up, grabbing for the reins of the nearest horse. More shots followed and the horse went down, kicking and squealing, while the other two skittered away from him.

Even though it would be foolish to be out here on foot, Jarrod also knew it was useless trying to mount up and ride out. Phillips would kill the remaining two horses to stop him doing so. And to try would be to waste precious time. Instead, Jarrod got up and ran, crouched over, towards where the line of trees marked the slope of the hill. If he could get amongst them he would be hidden and safe for a few precious moments.

Several shots followed, kicking up spouts of dust all round him. Just as he reached the trees he glanced back. Two horsemen had emerged into the open. Not looking where he was going he stepped forward and tripped on the roots of a tree. He fell heavily. Feet and hands scrabbled uselessly for a hold, arms and legs flailed. He tumbled over and over, rolling down the hillside, unable to stop himself.

Two more innocent dead men, Wincott thought in some despair, as they came to the shelf of land. Two dead soldiers. All right for Phillips to say they were Yankees and didn't count. Even if the posse from Sweetwater Crossing gave up chasing them, even if no lawmen came after them for the deputy, the army would be on their trail.

And all because Phillips had recognized their prisoner as someone called Jarrod Kilkline. At first, Wincott thought Phillips wanted to rescue the young man; but it seemed he wanted to do so for dark reasons of his own.

While Curtis and Ryan stayed with Melvin, Wincott and Phillips stood together at the point where Jarrod had fallen. The bottom of the hill was a long way below and through the trees and thick undergrowth no movement could be seen.

'He's dead.'

'Might not be. The bastard might be hurt bad, but alive mebbe.'

'He ain't.'

'I'm goin' down there, find out for sure.'

'Leave it, Harry. We ain't got time for all this.'

'The bastard betrayed me. I'm goin' after him. You can do whatever you like. But don't forget, Craig, in the circumstances you need me more'n I need you.' And Phillips started his horse down the steep slope.

Wincott turned round, signalling the others to come down, and, shrugging resignedly, because unfortunately the man was right, went after Phillips.

Jarrod lay, collapsed and breathless, jammed up against the trunk of a pine tree. His whole body hurt. There were bleeding scratches on his face and hands, and his jacket was torn. Groaning he sat up, and had to lean against the tree as pain speared his side so badly he felt sick.

Trembling, he put his head in his hands and the next time he looked up Harry Phillips was approaching him, a cocky grin on his face and a spring in his step.

Sweetwater Crossing was quiet as everyone attended the funerals of its two murdered citizens.

The town's dead were buried in a plot of land at the foot of the hills. It was planned to one day build a church to go with the cemetery. Now there was no church, no preacher. Old Bart, as well as acting as undertaker, had to take charge of the actual burials and speak words from the Bible over the graves.

On one side of the double grave, Sally was by Mrs Newley, the two women gaining some comfort from each other and the fact that Deputy Newley had loved them both.

On the opposite side, Glenda stood with Mrs Ericson, arm around her, heart full of sadness as she looked at the three Ericson children. She was unable to take in what had happened. It had been so fast, so unnecessary. And what would happen to them now? Would Mrs Ericson be able to run the store without her husband? Would she want to? Perhaps she would sell the place and return East to her family.

Old Bart finished his prayer and looked up, a fierce stare on his face. 'This is maybe the saddest day Sweetwater Crossing has ever known, but one thing is for sure, with Captain Butler out heading the posse . . .' Glenda wondered what Lester Peabody would say to that, 'the bastards, excuse me ladies, who did this will soon be caught and returned to face their just punishment.'

'String 'em up,' someone muttered, and there were other nods of agreement.

As Old Bart, helped by a couple of other men, began to fill in the graves, Mrs Ericson turned to Glenda. Clinging to her arm, she said, 'Oh, Glenda, what am I do?'

'You must be brave for the sake of the children.'

'You won't leave me alone, will you?'

'No,' Glenda said. 'I'll stay with you.'

'Well, well, hallo Jarrod, we meet again.' Phillips strode up to Jarrod giving him a hefty kick in the ribs. 'Hoped I'd catch up with you one day.'

'I seem to remember you caught up with me in the Chiricahua Mountains, but you ran away when I killed your Indian friends.'

Jarrod hoped he didn't sound as scared, or as hurt, as he felt.

Phillips laughed. 'Well you know what they say. How it's best to run away and live to fight another day.'

'So now you call shooting down an unarmed man fighting?'

'Sonofabitch asked for it. Same as you.' Phillips kicked Jarrod several more times.

With no choice but to put up with it, Jarrod curled

himself up in a tight ball, hoping it wouldn't last too long and that he wouldn't give Phillips the satisfaction of fainting.

As three other men rode up, Phillips was stopped by Wincott.

'Leave him alone. That posse is too damn close and we've got Melvin to think about.'

Phillips said something very uncomplimentary about both the posse and Melvin. All the same he stopped kicking Jarrod and leant down to drag him up by his coat collar.

His grin was evil as he said, 'You're comin' with me. I'll get the chance for some fun some time real soon. Mebbe more'n once. And then I'll shoot you down for the traitor you are.'

Then he shoved Jarrod forward so hard, he sprawled on his hands and face.

'Lucky for me you've got handcuffs on, saves me the trouble of tying you up. Now, come on, get up, like the man said we ain't got all day.'

FIFTEEN

'Look!' Butler pointed down the hill. 'Something's happened.'

Peabody rode up to where the other man had come to a halt. On a ledge below them he could see three horses, one of which was dead, and two unmoving figures on the ground, both wearing army blue. 'Let's get on down,' he said urgently.

Butler couldn't believe what he saw when they got there. Campbell and Thomas were dead and their prisoner no longer in evidence.

'The bastard!' he exclaimed. 'The bastard. I'll skin him alive when I find him.'

'You think Kilkline did this?'

Butler stopped pacing up and down to face Peabody. 'Of course, don't you?'

'He's not a killer.' Peabody considered himself a good judge of character. Jarrod might kill in self-defence but not in cold blood.

Butler snorted disbelievingly. 'He killed Corporal

McLane. Besides, who else could have done it?'

'Phillips and the gang?'

'Why?'

'I don't think Phillips needs an excuse, good or otherwise, to kill people. Think about it. Where did Kilkline get a gun? How did he get the drop on the troopers? Don't forget they would have been watching him carefully. Why shoot one horse and leave the other two here? He'd surely have ridden away, not walked. And if you look carefully you'll find these two men have been killed by a rifle, fired from somewhere up the hill where we were following the gang's tracks.'

Butler studied the ground and finally, reluctantly, had to agree with Peabody. 'All right, so where is Kilkline now? I bet he's joined up with his old pal and the rest of the gang.'

But Peabody was doubtful about that as well. As far as he could tell there was no love lost between the two men and Jarrod was scared of Phillips.

All the same where exactly had he gone?

Just at that moment Mr Marsh called to him from over by the trees. 'Here, Mr Peabody, I've found something.'

Scuffed ground, the tracks of horses, and the fact that someone had taken a tumble down the hill.

Peabody said, 'They've gone this way.'

Jarrod rode along behind Curtis Wincott. His body ached all over from both his fall and the kicking Phillips had given him, but more than that he was frightened. Capture by Lester Peabody, imprisonment by the army, paled into insignificance against being held by Harry Phillips.

Harry was going to kill him, very slowly, no doubt using some of the tricks he'd learned while gun-running to the Apaches. He'd take great delight in doing so, and the men with him, even if they were bothered, wouldn't dare try and stop him, for it was obvious that while they didn't like Phillips they were also scared of and overawed by him. Phillips had that effect on people.

'Hey, see that, up ahead,' Curtis Wincott said.

A spiral of smoke could clearly be seen rising above the treetops. It could mean anything: a cowboys' camp, Indians, or, maybe, a sodbuster's cabin. It did mean some sort of shelter.

Wincott stared across at Phillips. 'Let's just take it easy, no violence.'

' 'Course not,' Phillips agreed, with an innocent grin. 'Lessen it's necessary.'

Before long they came to a man-made clearing in the trees. Amongst the tree stumps was a small log cabin. It was in good shape, with a porch in front and well-fitting shutters on its windows. Logs were neatly stacked along one side and at the rear was a corral in which two ponies grazed.

'Help is at hand.' Phillips slid off his horse. He came over to Jarrod, grabbed his jacket, hauling him to the ground, then marched him up to the cabin's front door.

'Harry,' Wincott called in warning. 'Remember what I said.'

Phillips took no notice. Pausing only to draw his gun, he kicked the door open and shoved Jarrod inside.

Jarrod was propelled across the floor by Phillips's hefty push. He hit a low table and both he and it crashed to the floor.

A woman cried out in shock and a man demanded, 'What's going on?'

The couple who were sitting at a table jumped up in surprise at the abrupt entrance of Phillips into their lives.

From where he'd landed on the floor, Jarrod saw they were probably in their mid-forties but they looked older and careworn from living as poor, hard-working farmers. Both had grey hair, lined faces and dirt-encrusted hands. All the same, their home was as cared for inside as out with sturdy, home-made furniture, rag rugs on the floor and newspaper advertisements providing colour on the walls.

A fire burned brightly in the fireplace above which rested a shotgun. The man eyed the gun, but Phillips gave him no chance to reach it.

'Shut up! Sit down and behave yourselves. We need help; you're goin' to give it to us!'

As the other four came in, the man, realizing there was no way he could fight them all, collapsed down by his wife. He held her hand, while she murmured, 'My, oh my,' in a stunned way.

'What are your names?' Wincott asked.

'Earl and Jane Hopkins,' the man stuttered.

'Well, Earl, we don't mean you no harm.'

But the couple had seen Phillips and obviously didn't believe Wincott's reassurances.

'Yeah and don't worry about ol' Jarrod here,' Phillips said, kicking out at Jarrod's legs. 'He might be in handcuffs but he don't pose no threat. I'm keeping a real good eye on him!'

'All we want is somewhere to shelter up for a while,' Wincott said, 'some food to eat and some help for this poor wounded boy. Can you do that?'

Jane Hopkins might be terrified, but her heart was touched by the sight of Melvin, who was being supported by Curtis and Ryan. His face was splotched grey and red, while blood had soaked through to his jacket. Apart from little moans he made no sound.

'The poor boy,' she said. 'Bring him in to the bedroom.'

'Can you doctor him?' Ryan asked.

'I can make him comfortable, but I think that's all anyone can do for him.'

Ryan cast a look of disgust at Phillips, who took no notice.

Amidst the confusion of Melvin being carried into the bedroom and Jane gathering together bandages and water, Jarrod managed to go up to Earl Hopkins.

'Be careful,' he warned.

'Are they lawmen?' Hopkins sounded doubtful,

but was clearly influenced by the fact that Jarrod was in handcuffs.

'Hardly! They've just robbed the general store in Sweetwater Crossing and left two men dead. The one you've got to watch out for is the long-haired one, Harry Phillips.'

'And what's your story, son?'

'A long one. Let's just say I'm in even more trouble than you.'

'Hey you two!' Phillips yelled. 'Get away from one another. Don't want you planning any trouble. Ol' man, why don't you make yourself useful by fixing us somethin' to eat. We're all starving.'

'Best do as he says.'

'I can tell that for myself, son.'

'And hurry it up.'

'Do you want any help?'

'No, Jarrod, he surely don't. You stay where I can keep an eye on you. Don't want you gettin' any ideas about escaping.'

From over by the bedroom door, Craig Wincott sighed. It was settling down to be another long, awkward afternoon for his gang.

Sergeant Cook lifted his hand bringing the troop of cavalry to a halt. The hostiles' trail had petered out some way back and, although Cook was a good tracker, he hadn't found it again. The hostiles had disappeared as hostiles often did, and were probably on their way back to their camp somewhere in the mountains.

'Are we going after 'em?' Corporal Hacknell asked.

Cook shook his head. 'It won't do any good. It would take too long and if we do find the camp how can we tell which of the Indians there are the hostiles we're searching for?'

Some commanding officers might approve of all the Indians being lumped together and shot, just on the off chance that some of them were hostiles. Major Sanderson wasn't like that. He was quite prepared for the Indians to be chased down and captured or killed, but only if they were guilty.

Neither was there any sign of the gang of robbers meant to be in the area.

'What shall we do?' Hacknell asked.

'Perhaps it'll be best to go back to Fort Ludlow, find out if Major Sanderson knows any more, get new orders.'

'Yeah, OK.'

'Get one of the troopers to ride back with a message. Tell the major we ain't had any luck and we're on our way.'

SIXTEEN

'They're goin' to kill us, ain't they, son?' Earl Hopkins asked Jarrod.

'Craig Wincott, that's the oldest one, won't want to, but if Phillips decides on it he won't be able to stop him.'

'And that's what Phillips will decide?'

Jarrod could see little point in lying to the couple, or giving them false hope. 'Wouldn't be at all surprised.' Wearily he leant back resting his head against the table leg to which he was tied.

Earl and Jane Hopkins were tied to two of the other legs. They were in the kitchen. Through the closed door they could hear the gang in the parlour. They'd long since finished the meal Hopkins had cooked for them and had now started on the bottle of whiskey he kept for medicinal purposes.

'Oh dear, why is this happening to us?' Jane asked, tears squeezing out of the corners of her eyes. 'We're just here minding our own business, trying to earn a living. And then they arrive. It isn't fair.'

'Now, now, Jane, we ain't been hurt so far,' her husband tried to comfort her. 'And you know a lot of things in this life ain't fair. It's up to us to do something about it.'

'What can we do?'

'Jarrod, how long do you think they'll stay here?'

'Not much longer than the morning. There's a posse on their trail, led by a man who won't give up. They'll want to be on their way. With or without their injured companion.'

Jane shook her head. 'He was hurt badly. I doubt he'll be alive come morning. Poor boy.'

Hopkins grunted. 'We must consider ourselves, not any of them. So you think we've got till morning to do something?'

'Yeah,' Jarrod agreed, with no real idea of what they could do.

Craig Wincott stood up, stretched. The others were asleep; Phillips in a chair, Curtis and Ryan on the floor by the fire. But sleep was far away from Wincott. He was worried. How was this going to turn out? Events had taken on a momentum of their own and he seemed powerless to stop them.

He went into the bedroom where Melvin lay in the Hopkins's bed. The boy was still alive, but barely, his breath shallow and painful and, despite all the woman's efforts, the wound in his side wouldn't stop bleeding. Melvin was dying and there wasn't a damn thing he could do about it.

Jarrod had no way of escaping from the handcuffs, but maybe he could loosen the rope Phillips had used to tie his wrists to the table leg. The table was home-made and quite old with several splinters. He could rub the rope against a splinter and hopefully it would break.

Phillips, the bastard, had tied the rope as tightly as he could, more or less cutting off circulation in Jarrod's hands. After a while his wrists were torn so raw they started to bleed. Ignoring the pain, he continued rubbing. After almost an hour he was rewarded. The rope frayed and snapped. Cautiously he got to his feet. He had no idea of the time but through the window he could see it was still dark outside. Phillips and the others wouldn't be expecting their prisoners to try to escape. There must be time to get away.

Earl and Jane Hopkins were asleep. For a moment Jarrod wondered about leaving them, making good his own escape. But he couldn't do that. Jane was right; what was happening to them wasn't fair, nor their fault. Quickly, he went up to Hopkins, shaking him, putting a hand over the man's mouth.

'Hush,' he whispered close to his ear. 'I'm free. I'll untie you. You help your wife. Understand?'

Hopkins gave a quick nod.

*

Wincott sat by the bed, holding Melvin's hand. The boy groaned once or twice but never regained consciousness. Around three in the morning his breath rattled in his throat and he died.

Wincott sighed. It was over. Melvin had never spoken of any folks and he wondered if the boy had anyone worrying about him.

'Can you both ride?'

'Of course we can,' Earl said, a bit scornfully.

'Head for Sweetwater Crossing. You'll be safe there.'

'What about you?' Jane put a hand on Jarrod's arm.

'Don't worry about me.' Jarrod had no intention of going back to the town. 'You two just worry about yourselves.' He went to the kitchen door, which no one had bothered to lock. 'Let's go.'

When Wincott went back into the parlour, Harry Phillips was awake, standing rigidly by the window as if he was at attention, looking out at the dark night.

'He's dead,' Craig announced to the man's back. 'So that's one problem we don't have to worry about, ain't it?'

Phillips swung round. 'Hey now, ain't no call to be so nasty. Melvin knew the risks when he joined the outlaw trail. The one to blame is that Eastern dude who shot him.'

Wincott was too tired and dispirited to argue. It

wouldn't do any good. Phillips didn't accept any blame or guilt over his actions. Sometimes he didn't even seem to know where he was any more and spoke as if he was still in the army fighting the war.

'We'll leave in the morning. And, Harry, we leave the Hopkinses alive when we go.'

'If you say so.'

But Wincott didn't believe his assurances and wondered if the morning was when he would have to go up against Phillips. He didn't want to because he knew what the outcome would be. Phillips was fast, accurate and deadly: Wincott wasn't.

'We'll have to saddle and bridle our ponies,' Hopkins said, as they went into the corral, where the gang's horses now grazed as well. 'Jane can't ride otherwise.'

Jarrod didn't want to hang around; he didn't particularly want to wait around for the Hopkinses. He wanted to get on a horse and ride away.

'Will you help us?' Jane asked.

Jarrod sighed. 'Let's be as quick as we can.'

The saddles and bridles hung from the corral walls, because out here they didn't usually need to worry about thieves. Jarrod picked up one of the saddles, flinging it over the back of the nearest pony, which gave a little whicker of surprise. While he did up the girth, Hopkins did his best to secure the bridle, but the man was nervous, trembling, communicating his anxiety to the animal, which shifted about, making everything take twice as long.

'What was that?' Phillips looked up sharply.
'What?'
'I thought I heard one of the horses.'
'I didn't hear anythin'.'
'Those bastards ain't tryin' to escape, are they?'
'How could they? You tied 'em up yourself.'

'Are you ready?' Jarrod asked anxiously.

'Yeah. We'll have to ride back to the trail at the front of the cabin. Ain't no way through the trees, not in the dark anyway.'

'All right.'

'What about you?'

'I can ride bare-back.' Jarrod thought they'd been lucky so far. He didn't want to push it. He helped Jane up in the saddle. 'Just go.' He smacked the animal hard on the rump. As it darted forward he swung up on Phillips's horse. He dug heels in the animal's side, following the Hopkinses around the side of the house.

'Goddammit! It is them! They're gettin' away.' Phillips paused only to kick a surprised Curtis out of the way and to grab up his rifle before he was flinging himself out of the door.

'Don't shoot,' Wincott yelled.

But Phillips had already plunged off the porch and sent several shots towards the fleeing Hopkinses.

None hit them. Yelling with rage, the man ran forward, but the darkness had swallowed up the couple and he no longer had a target to shoot at.

Then, from close behind him, he heard another horse. Quickly he swung round.

Jarrod!

Phillips didn't bother trying to shoot, didn't want to shoot to kill. That would make it too easy on the traitor. Instead he took a step back, hefted the rifle by its barrel and knocked Jarrod off the horse's back.

SEVENTEEN

Phillips swung at the horse, stopping its all-out gallop and would have vaulted on to its back to give chase had Wincott not stopped him.

'We've gotta go after them!' Harry screamed.

'You can't follow 'em in the dark.'

'We must stop them.'

'Why?'

Phillips looked at the other man as if he couldn't believe his ears. 'They know who we are. They can identify us.'

'So can nearly all of Sweetwater Crossing, so I don't see that it matters much. Leave it, Harry, they can't do us any harm.'

'What about this little bastard?' Phillips strode over to Jarrod, who lay winded and hurt on the ground. Phillips kicked him several times. 'Bastard! Trying to escape. Helping those two.'

Jarrod rolled out of the way of the man's feet.

'Leave him now,' Wincott said.

Phillips strode away, a sulky look of exasperation on his face.

Wincott looked at Jarrod and shrugged. Jarrod knew that while the man had stopped Phillips this time he wouldn't risk the man's wrath by helping Jarrod any more. Jarrod was on his own.

'What are we goin' to do?' Curtis asked his brother.

'Get out of here as soon as it gets light.' Wincott looked up at the sky. That would be in about an hour's time. 'Meantime, we'll raid the cupboards and make us some breakfast.'

'What about Melvin?' Ryan asked.

'There's nothing we can do for him now.'

'We oughta at least bury him.'

'We ain't got time.'

'Don't matter much to Melvin,' Phillips said. 'He's dead. As for you, Kilkline, I'll see you in hell.'

'Do tell.' Jarrod was getting fed up with Phillips's threats and wasn't exactly happy that he'd helped the others get away and here he was still a prisoner. He was in danger of losing his own temper.

'You two can work out your problems later on when we've dodged the posse,' Wincott said, with a heavy sigh. 'Meanwhile come on inside and get something to eat. Then we head out.'

'Someone's coming.' Peabody put down his cup of coffee and sat up straight, hand going to his gun.

Butler got to his feet and went to the edge of the

little camp. Damn these trees, it made it impossible to see a thing. 'Two riders,' he announced, as Peabody and the rest of the posse joined him.

'Is it them?' Mr Marsh asked anxiously.

A few moments later two horses came crashing out of the trees. At once they all saw it wasn't the men they were after but, surprisingly, a man and a woman, both of whom looked frightened.

'Stop there!' Peabody called out, stepping into the path of the horses and raising his hands.

'Jesus,' Butler mumbled. The man was going to get himself killed one of these days.

But evidently Peabody knew what he was doing. While the woman cried out in fear, the man leant across catching hold of the reins of her horse and pulled both mounts to a halt.

'Thank God,' he said. 'You must be the posse those men spoke about.'

Earl and Jane Hopkins sat with Peabody and Butler by the camp-fire, drinking coffee and eating bacon and beans.

'I was sure we were going to be killed,' Jane said, still in a state of shock, unable to believe everything that had happened.

'We would have been if it hadn't been for Jarrod.'

'So he was with them,' Butler said, with a triumphant look at Peabody.

But his triumph was short lived as Hopkins added, 'He was their prisoner. In handcuffs.'

'The handcuffs are mine,' Peabody said wryly.

'Well, they made no effort to take them off him. And last night he was tied up just as we were.'

'And he looked as if someone had beaten him,' Jane added. 'Poor boy.'

'How did he help you?' Butler asked.

'Somehow he managed to get free from his ropes and he got us free as well. He helped us with the ponies.'

'He was right behind us,' Jane said.

'Well, where is he now?'

'He might have got away too, ridden in the other direction but, Mr Butler, I think they must have caught him. They certainly realized we were getting away because they shot at us. Luckily we weren't hit. Jarrod might have been.'

'The poor boy,' Jane repeated. 'I don't like to think of him in their hands. And there was another poor boy with them who was shot bad. They wanted my help with him, but I couldn't save him. He was dying.'

'Did they say anything about where they were going? What they were doing?' Peabody wasted no time in sympathy for the young man he'd shot. Those who insisted on living by the gun sometimes died by it too.

'One of 'em mentioned Utah,' Hopkins said.

'Perhaps it doesn't matter.' Butler reached out to refill their coffee cups. 'We're not that far behind.'

'That you ain't,' Hopkins agreed with a nod. 'Our

place is just over the ridge.'

Peabody asked, 'Mr Hopkins, what do you want to do? We'll have to go on to your farm, follow the trail from there. Do you want to carry on into Sweetwater Crossing or accompany us back to your place?'

The couple looked at one another and Jane said, 'Those men won't still be there will they?'

'Not if they've got any sense.'

'They know a posse is after them,' Butler added. 'They'll want to be on their way.'

'What about that poor dying boy? Surely they won't leave him?'

'I'm betting they will,' Peabody said. 'If he's alive we might be able to help him. If he's dead we can bury him.'

'I don't like being driven from my own home,' Hopkins said. 'But, Jane, it's up to you.'

'If you really think it'll be safe. . . .' Her voice petered out.

'We'll come back with you.'

'Let's get going then,' Peabody said. 'And, everyone, we're getting close. I don't need to tell you all to be careful, do I?' He emptied his cup of the dregs of coffee and stood up, ready for action.

Major Alan Sanderson stood at his office window, staring out at the empty parade-ground. Soon reveille would be blown and the troopers would gather there for their morning inspection. Already he could see movement at the back of the stables.

His face was creased with a frown of worry.

Troopers Campbell and Thomas should have been back with their prisoner long before this. Although young they were experienced men. He couldn't believe that one Southern boy would be a match for them. But Captain Butler had warned him, not about Jarrod Kilkline, but about the bounty hunter; he hadn't listened.

Perhaps something had gone wrong in Sweetwater Crossing.

Sergeant Cook should be back real soon. The messenger he'd despatched had arrived to say the patrol was returning to the fort. Once he got here, Sanderson determined to send his sergeant and some men into town – sort all this out. He wasn't about to let a bounty hunter deprive the army of trying someone who'd killed one of its own.

In the middle of the posse, Earl and Jane Hopkins approached the return to their home nervously. To their relief the horses were gone and there was no sign of the gang. No one, except for the dead Melvin Stack lying in the bedroom.

'They didn't even take the time to bury the poor boy,' Jane said, with tears in her eyes.

'No, but they took time to take everything they could carry,' Earl added.

'They've gone and won't be back, that's the main thing,' Peabody assured them. 'You've nothing more to worry about. Mr Marsh, see to the horses, make sure they're watered. You two, take the body and bury it, somewhere out of sight of the cabin. These folks don't want to be reminded of what happened here any more than they have to be.'

While everyone did the man's bidding, and Butler helped Earl and Jane tidy up indoors, Peabody roamed about outside. There was no sign of any blood so if Kilkline had been caught, as the Hopkinses feared, and hadn't escaped, as Peabody feared, then presumably he hadn't been shot.

He then followed the trail of the gang's horses from the corral to where they had reached the road and turned away from Sweetwater Crossing.

'Any luck?' Butler asked coming up behind him.

'Plenty of sign. I suppose they're in too much of a hurry to try and hide it at the moment. We can take advantage of their haste.'

'OK. We'll start out in a few minutes then. Will Earl and Jane be all right on their own or should we leave a couple of men with them?'

'I'd rather have everyone with me. We're getting close; I don't want any mistakes made.'

When asked, Earl felt the same way. He said, 'Go get the bastards.'

Peabody nodded. 'We'll do our best.'

EIGHTEEN

'This looks as good a place as any,' Phillips said, drawing his horse to a halt and swinging down out of the saddle.

He'd come to a halt at the top of a hill. A line of rocks ranged along it. Below him the slope was almost bare of trees.

'A good place for what?' Wincott asked suspiciously.

'To ambush the damn posse, what else?' Phillips stood, hands on hips staring up at the other men. 'The posse that is on our trail if you remember.'

'We can outrun it.'

'No, we can't. They won't give up and they're catching up on us.' Phillips didn't say that was partly because, wanting a fight, he was making it easy for them. 'We should never have stopped at that farm.'

Wincott thought he could also point out they shouldn't have wasted time chasing after Jarrod Kilkline, but he kept quiet.

'Harry's right,' Curtis said, unhappy at having to agree with the man.

' 'Course I am. Look, Craig, you weren't the one pulled the trigger on those two men back in town and, Christ, you've been whining about it ever since, but if you're caught you face the hangman same as me. So does Curtis. Do you want to see your brother die and know you could have done something to stop it?'

Wincott didn't. Neither did he want to shoot it out with the posse, but right then there didn't seem much choice. 'OK, we'll make a stand here.'

'How far behind them are we, do you think?' Butler said, as the posse came to a halt at the bottom of a hill. He took a drink of water from his canteen.

Peabody studied the tracks, a worried frown creasing his face. Since leaving the Hopkins's farm the gang hadn't bothered to try and hide their trail. Nor were they hurrying. He wondered if they were getting careless or whether there was some other reason for their actions.

'An hour or so. They went up that hill.' Peabody didn't like the look of it.

'What's the matter?'

'Now we're out of the trees without much cover there are several places would make a good spot for an ambush.'

'You reckon they'll try that?'

'Maybe.'

'They won't just keep running?'

'I have my doubts about Phillips. According to accounts of his service in the Civil War, he was a good leader of his men. He was also the kind to fight first and retreat later. He'll know we're still coming after him and will want to do something about it.'

'I was a good leader as well.'

'But were you dangerous? Watch yourself is all I'm saying.'

'They're comin'.' Phillips had excitement in his voice. 'Get ready.'

Jarrod lay on the ground next to Harry, wondering what to do, wondering what he *could* do. He didn't want to help the posse and find himself once more a prisoner of either Peabody or Butler, yet neither did he want to see them killed; or to remain in Phillips's hands.

He watched as the posse – Peabody and Butler at the head of the four or five men – made a slow way up the hill. He looked at the Wincotts and Tom Ryan. They might not like this any more than he did, but their lives were at stake if they let themselves be taken. They would shoot to kill the same as Harry. And one look at Harry's face told him that the man couldn't wait to start shooting.

He couldn't just let those men ride into an ambush.

Everyone watched the posse. No one was watching him.

Suddenly Jarrod leapt to his feet, yelling and waving his arms.

'What the. . . ?' Phillips swung round. 'You sonofabitch!' For a moment his finger tightened on the trigger of his gun. Then he changed his mind. 'Killing you would be too easy,' he snarled and, getting to his feet, clattered into Jarrod knocking him down. He jammed his gun into Jarrod's stomach. 'Stay down, you bastard, and shut up.'

'It's too late,' Wincott said. 'They've seen us.'

And when Jarrod next looked he saw that the posse had dismounted and scattered, finding what shelter they could amongst the boulders and few trees on the hillside.

At Jarrod's yell, Peabody called out 'Dismount!' He flung himself off his horse, darting behind a rock, pulling out his gun as he did so.

'Was that Kilkline?' Butler asked from nearby.

'Sounded like it.'

'Why would he help us?'

'I told you he's not a cold-blooded killer and nor is he going willingly along with Phillips.'

'What do you want to do?'

Peabody looked round. The choice was between going back to the bottom of the hill or continuing to the top. The ridge made a good place to shoot at the posse from, but, who knew, if they gave up now, the gang might find a better place from which to stage an ambush; or even get away.

'Butler, why don't you and me climb the hill while the others lay down a covering fire?'

'Just what I was going to suggest.'

'Wouldn't it be best to get on our way now they've seen us?' Wincott said.

'No.' Phillips reached out a hand to stop him getting to his feet. 'We make a stand here and now.' He wasn't about to give up the chance of a gunfight.

There was no further time for argument as the men below began to fire. Bullets sang off rocks, causing vicious ricochets, or ploughed harmlessly into the earth, but came nowhere near. The horses whinnied and fidgeted with fright.

'What are they doin'?' Ryan asked. 'They can't hope to hit us from all that way down there.'

'They ain't tryin' to,' Phillips said scornfully. 'They're providing cover. Look! There's one of the bastards.' He raised his gun and fired.

'You missed,' Jarrod jeered.

'You shut up. I won't miss you.'

'There's another 'un.' Ryan raised himself up a little in order to get a better view.

'Get down,' Wincott said.

It was too late. Below, Butler saw the movement. He stopped, aimed and fired. The bullet caught Ryan in the neck. Blood sprayed out around him and he fell sideways, rolled over once, kicked his heels and died.

'Oh God,' Curtis moaned.

'Keep firing at 'em,' Phillips ordered. 'We're in a good position here. We can beat the bastards.'

But while Phillips had a good position, he didn't have good men; or at least not men skilled in battle or with any heart in the fight.

Butler's next shot caught Curtis in the arm. The young man squealed in pain and, clutching the wound, he rolled away.

'Curtis!' Wincott cried. 'Are you OK?'

'I'm hurt. I'm bleeding.'

'For Chrissakes,' Phillips muttered in disgust. 'You ain't hurt that bad. It's a flesh wound.'

'You don't know that, you bastard. You're goin' to get us all killed.' Wincott holstered his gun and went over to his brother, relieved when he saw that the wound, although bloody, didn't seem to be too serious.

'Am I shot bad?' Curtis moaned.

'No. The bullet is still in your arm though and will have to come out. Can you make it to the horses?'

Phillips swung round pointing his gun at them. 'You two just stay where the hell you are. Goddamn cowards. I'll shoot you for sure you try anything.' He turned back. 'What are you grinning at?' he demanded of Jarrod. 'I can still beat all these bastards and then I'll deal with you.'

And Jarrod thought he might yet be able to carry out his threats. Phillips had plenty of ammunition, a good position as he said, and when he controlled his temper he was an excellent shot.

*

On the hill Peabody and Butler had almost reached the ridge. Peabody counted the shots and where they were fired from. It seemed to him only one man remained against them.

And when that man must have used up all the bullets in his gun and there was a gap in the firing, Peabody saw his chance – one sprint and he'd reach the ridge – and seized it.

But instead of reloading Phillips merely stooped and picked up the gun Ryan had dropped.

And as Peabody burst out into the open Phillips grinned, stood up and raised the gun.

At that distance he couldn't miss.

NINETEEN

'No!' Butler saw what was happening and cried out a warning.

'No!' Jarrod yelled and launched himself at Phillips even as the man pulled the trigger.

Peabody cried out and, with a surprised and scared look on his face, dropped to the ground as the bullet whined by his ear.

Jarrod and Phillips went down in a blur of arms and legs, kicking and punching. Phillips tried to hit Jarrod with the gun, or bring it round to shoot him. He was shouting and swearing while Jarrod clutched at the man's gunhand and clung on desperately.

'Curtis?' Wincott said. 'Let's get outa here!'

'What about Harry?'

'What about him? We don't owe him anythin'. He's nothin' but trouble. Can you ride?'

'Hell, yes, if it means gettin' away.'

Wincott pulled his brother to his feet and helped him over to the horses, pushing Curtis up into the saddle. He mounted his own animal and together they rode pell mell down the other side of the hill and out of harm's way.

Butler stood up. 'Come on,' he called and signalled for the other men of the posse to follow him. He scrambled up the hill, pausing to touch Peabody on the shoulder. 'You OK?'

'I'm not hit if that's what you mean.' But Peabody's heart was still pounding with the fright of staring death in the face. He still couldn't quite understand how he was alive.

However, he recovered quickly enough to be right behind Butler when he leapt up amongst the rocks.

Phillips and Jarrod were still struggling on the ground, Phillips gradually getting the upper hand.

'Make sure he's dead.' Peabody indicated Ryan. Then he dragged the two men apart, shoving Jarrod out of the way and hitting Phillips round the jaw.

The man went down, but when he rolled over he still had the gun in his hand. He would have tried to use it, except that now the other posse members were arriving on the scene.

Phillips knew when he was beaten. Grinning, he dropped the gun and raised his hands. 'I surrender.'

Peabody kicked the gun out of the way and secured Phillips's hands behind his back with a second pair of handcuffs. 'Give me an excuse and I'll shoot you.'

'Oh, I ain't about to do that, but I expect I'll get

my chance somewhere along the line. Who are you anyway? You don't look much to me.'

Everyone present could have told Phillips looks were deceiving.

'The name's Lester Peabody. And don't be so cocky. I've brought in better men than you and your poster says "Wanted, Dead or Alive", best remember that.'

Meanwhile Butler returned from making sure Tom Ryan was dead and he helped Jarrod to his feet. 'I guess even if he doesn't get around to thanking you, Peabody owes you his life. Why did you do it?'

Jarrod shrugged. 'Phillips was going to kill me the same as he was the rest of you.'

Peabody left Mr Marsh and the rest of the posse to keep an eye on Phillips and went over to stare down at the direction in which the Wincott brothers had ridden away. Far below were more trees, a stream running through them.

'Should we go after them?' Butler asked.

Perhaps with better, more experienced men in the posse Peabody would do so, for he didn't like the thought of any outlaw getting away. But the men weren't experienced. They were already tired; Mr Marsh was on the point of exhaustion. To prolong the chase might be to risk their lives, for if he could get careless and almost get shot, so could they. And they might not be so lucky.

Besides, Phillips had been the one to do the shooting and it was Phillips he wanted; Phillips he now had.

'Let's leave them. The army can go after them. The men want to get back home.'

'All right,' Butler nodded in agreement. He wanted to go home as well.

Wincott stopped at the bottom of the hill where the stream entered the trees and they couldn't be seen from above. He dismounted and helped Curtis from his horse, laying him on the ground. Gulping down some water from his canteen, he watched the members of the posse milling about on the hilltop and wondered if they would give chase. So far no one had made a move to do so. He couldn't really believe he and Curtis would be allowed to get away but maybe the posse was as weary as he was and was willing to be satisfied now Ryan was dead and they had Phillips.

Wincott turned back to his brother. 'It looks like we're safe for the moment. The first thing to do is get you to a doctor and have your arm seen to and then we ride to Utah.'

'Sounds good to me.'

'And then it'll be just the two of us again. Like before.'

Never, ever again did Wincott want to meet someone like Harry Phillips.

'You're not going to make trouble are you?' Butler said.

'Trouble?' Peabody sounded surprised.

'You said before you were after both Kilkline and Phillips. Now we've caught them perhaps you believe you should be on your way to Tucson with them.'

The thought had crossed Peabody's mind.

'Even allowing for the fact that I don't think you could handle both men . . .' Peabody thought he most certainly could, 'the army still has first call on Kilkline and the citizens of Sweetwater Crossing will have something to say about the right of trying and sentencing Phillips.'

Peabody frowned, not agreeing with that either. He had no wish to waste his time in going back to Sweetwater Crossing or in having to persuade either army or outraged citizenry of his right to both prisoners. Unfortunately, he could see no alternative. The posse would side with Butler and he couldn't argue with them all.

Anyway, it made sense. He needed supplies and more ammunition. To cross the desert with two prisoners without making the proper arrangements would be extremely foolish. He'd just have to wait and see what happened once he'd made those proper arrangements.

He went over to where Jarrod sat on the ground. 'We're starting back for town in a while. Once I've sorted things out there I'll be taking both you and Phillips back with me. Understand?'

Jarrod never failed to be amazed at the man's confidence in his own abilities; nor to doubt it.

Harry Phillips looked across at Jarrod and

laughed. 'Hey, Lieutenant, it don't look like your goddamn heroism in saving the life of that Yankee sonofabitch has done you much good. You're still in handcuffs same as me and you're still a prisoner same as me. I guess we're goin' to stand trial together!'

TWENTY

On their way back to Sweetwater Crossing, Jarrod rode up to where Peabody and Butler rode at the head of the posse. 'Mr Peabody, can I ask one thing of you?'

'What's that?'

'Please, don't put me in the jail cell with Harry. He'll kill me for certain.'

Peabody glanced across at the other man who rode along in the middle of the posse, lips pursed in a silent whistle as if he didn't have a care in the world. Phillips was mad, of course. He was also filled with a need for vengeance: against the law and the world in general and Jarrod in particular. Despite the handcuffs securing his hands behind his back he would doubtless try to find a way to hurt his one-time companion and might well succeed.

'I'll see what I can do.'

Jarrod breathed a sigh of relief. He'd been unsure whether for once the man would let his heart rule his head. It must have been a most unusual occurrence because Peabody looked very uncomfortable with his decision.

'Here.' Glenda handed Mrs Ericson a couple of tins of tomatoes. 'That's the last of them.'

Mrs Ericson stacked them on the shelf besides the rest, climbed down off the stool and shook out her skirts.

'Mrs Ericson, have you decided what you're going to do?' Glenda wondered what would happen if the woman said she was going back East to her family. Glenda had promised she would help the woman, stay with her and her children, would Mrs Ericson want her to go as well? She wouldn't want to go, but a promise was a promise.

'I've decided to stay here.'

Glenda let out the breath she'd been holding.

'Despite what happened, this is still a good place to live and bring up children. We have friends here. And although I'm sure my family would give me a home I'd only be a nuisance, living off their charity. Although it won't be easy, especially at first, at least here I can be my own woman and have a certain amount of freedom.'

'I'll help you all I can.'

'I know you will, dear. I don't know what I'd have done without you. But once Captain Butler gets back you'll have your own life to lead.'

Glenda hoped she was right.

The door opened and, as both women looked up, Old Bart poked his head into the store. 'Posse's coming back. They've got a couple of prisoners with 'em.'

Glenda took off her apron. 'Let's go and see.'

By the time the posse rode into Sweetwater Crossing quite a crowd had gathered, lining the sidewalk by the jail.

'Looks like we've got a welcoming committee,' Phillips said, sounding quite pleased.

In fact, Jarrod was sure he would have tipped his hat to the crowd if he could. At sight of him a few boos went up but the smile never left Phillips's face.

'Butler, can you handle him?' Peabody asked.

'Why? Where are you going?'

'To see if I can get Kilkline locked up someplace else, so he doesn't have to be with Phillips. Don't look so suspicious, I'm not running out on you.'

'OK.'

'And, Butler, leave the handcuffs on him. Don't take any chances.'

The other members of the posse hurried away to their homes, and Mr Marsh went to the store determined to be on his way as soon as the next stagecoach arrived – he thought Sweetwater Crossing was meant to be a quiet place!

Jarrod stood in the jailhouse office while Butler took Phillips through to the cell. He wondered about making a break for it but soon gave up on the idea; with so many people out on the street he wouldn't get far.

It wasn't long before Peabody returned. 'Come on,' he said, and took Jarrod down to the small office that served the stagecoach line. 'You can stay in here. It's got a strong lock on the door.'

Jarrod slumped down at the desk. Now what? Would he be handed over to the army again? If Peabody was going to take Phillips back to Tucson perhaps that might be best. Phillips was tricky. Crossing the desert he'd probably find plenty of opportunities for escape and in so doing kill anyone who got in his way.

Butler was pleased to see Glenda open the door and come into the office. 'Hello, sweetheart.'

'Come home.'

'I don't know.' Butler went to the window and looked out. The crowd was still on the streets, showing no sign of dispersing.

'It's nothing to do with you. Please, Myles.'

Against his better judgement, Butler allowed himself to be persuaded to leave the jailhouse. Once home he sat down and took off his boots, while Glenda busied herself making him coffee.

'You look tired.'

'I am. It was a long chase and Peabody kept up a fast pace. He might look weedy but he's about the most determined man I've ever met. How are you? How's it been here?'

Glenda made a face, putting his coffee down on

the table. 'Not very good, although Mrs Ericson is coping quite well. Mrs Newley has decided to leave town. She's got a sister in Denver and is going to live with her. Myles, what's going to happen now?'

'With the two men locked up here, you mean?'

'Yes.'

'Well, Kilkline is still wanted by the army. And I'm betting Major Sanderson will send some men here to see why his two troopers never made it back to the fort.'

'Yes, we've heard that a troop of cavalry is on its way.'

'Well, then they can take Kilkline with them. Phillips will have to stay here until Sheriff Beale arrives. Then it'll be up to him to decide what to do. Whether to call in a circuit judge or take him elsewhere to stand trial. Peabody won't like either but he'll have to put up with it.'

'And you? What are you going to do?'

'Me?' Butler sounded surprised. 'Like you said it's nothing to do with me.'

'The two Wincott brothers are still out there.'

Butler's face darkened at the thought of them getting away with the robbery but all he said was, 'I'm going to set up my carpentry business again. Be with you. Do all the things we talked about before I went away.' Glenda said nothing. 'Don't you want that?'

'Of course I do.'

'Then what's the matter? Why the worried look?'

Glenda sat down opposite him. 'It's simply that I

can't see you settling into your old way of life and being content.'

'Yes I will; it's what I want.'

'Are you sure?'

'Yes.'

She reached across, stroking his arms. 'You were eager to join the posse.'

'I had to. You know that. If I remember aright you wanted me to go.'

'Can you promise me you won't go away again?'

'It's not fair of you to ask something like that, Glenda. Sometimes duty comes first.'

'Is it just about duty? You've been away from Sweetwater Crossing; you've been involved in battles, commanded men, won medals. I think that as well as duty it's now about excitement and the fact that your old way of life can't give you what you need.'

'That's not true.'

'Isn't it?'

Butler didn't reply. Was Glenda right? Surely he'd had enough of tracking down the enemy and of fighting? Surely he could find a life here in town?

'I'd understand if you didn't want me any more either.' There were tears in her eyes.

'Oh, Glenda, no.' He got up and went round to the girl, pulling her to her feet, taking her into his arms. 'I love you. I always will. It's really more a matter of whether you can put up with me and the things I do.'

Glenda bit her lip. 'I'm not sure I could understand or cope with you always riding away, knowingly taking risks, not sure if you'd come back.'

'But I won't be doing that. I'll be here with you.' Butler's heart was pounding. He couldn't lose Glenda, not now when he'd just found her again. 'You don't have to worry. I love you. I've had enough of fighting.'

Glenda didn't look convinced. Myles obviously meant what he said, while he was saying it, but she wasn't altogether sure he would be able to keep his word.

The trouble was, in his heart, Myles wasn't sure he could either.

TWENTY-ONE

Jarrod stood at the window, staring out. All afternoon, people had stayed on the streets, wandering up and down, gathering in small groups. Voices were raised in anger. The saloon had done a roaring trade. A few men had passed the stagecoach office, looking in. They knew he was in there. Did they also know that Jarrod had nothing to do with the robbery and murders? Would they listen to anyone who told them so?

He didn't want to die, especially for something he hadn't done. And, if it came to it, would he die bravely and strongly or begging for his life?

Peabody wouldn't let a mob lynch him. But if no one helped him could even Peabody handle a mob all by himself?

Anyway where was Peabody? He'd always turned up before when he wasn't wanted; now he was wanted where the hell was he?

*

If Harry Phillips was worried he didn't show it. He sat down on the straw, got himself as comfortable as possible and went to sleep.

Sergeant Cook brought his small troop of men to a halt at a waterhole surrounded by trees. He felt they deserved a rest. They'd been out with him chasing hostiles, returned to the fort, only to start out again almost immediately for Sweetwater Crossing.

Dammit he felt like a rest!

And what could be so important at Sweetwater Crossing that they needed to put blisters on their butts for? If anything had happened to Campbell and Thomas it had happened by now – nothing they could do about it. Jarrod Kilkline would be caught sooner or later.

As for the gang of robbers – well, Cook was an army man, they were a civilian matter, let the law deal with them.

'We'll stop here for an hour, rest the horses, have something to eat. Then we'll be on our way.'

'Why should we have to wait till the law gets here? It might be weeks before Sheriff Beale comes back.'

'We don't even know where he is.'

'And he might take Phillips for trial someplace else where he might get off.'

'The army . . .' Old Bart said.

'The army ain't gonna help us. They don't take any interest in what goes on here.'

'I don't know about this. We've never done anythin' like this before.'

Old Bart was shouted down.

'That's because nothin' like this has ever happened here.'

'Do you want the bastard freed?'

'He's a robber and killer. He don't deserve nothin' better.'

'He should be hanged.'

Of course, Old Bart thought the same. He just didn't like the idea of taking the law into their own hands, doing something they might regret come morning. But the others were determined. They were all hot-headed; a lot of drink had been consumed. God knew what would they would do without him to lead them. They needed him.

'And when we've seen to Phillips we'll go after the Wincotts. Show these outlaws they can't come into our town and rob it and expect to get away with it!'

'Yeah.' There was general agreement about that as well.

'OK,' Old Bart agreed. 'But we must do it right.'

Sally stood at the door of the saloon staring at the mob across the street. She didn't like the look of this. Where was Lester Peabody? He'd know what to do. But she hadn't seen him since he'd returned to town with the posse. She sighed. She wasn't the sort of girl men visited during the day.

The man called Harry Phillips was in the jail. He was the one who had shot Deputy Newley down like a dog. But while Phillips deserved to die for what he'd done, he didn't deserve to die at the hands of a mob. Sally had witnessed a lynch mob in action in the last town where she'd worked; it had been horrible, something she didn't want to see again. The army was on its way, but the soldiers wouldn't arrive in time to stop this.

She had to do something.

Captain Butler! He'd know what to do and she knew where he lived.

Even as she made her decision, the mob, with no one and nothing to stop them, surged towards the jail. There was no time to waste.

Picking up her skirts, Sally ran down the street.

TWENTY-TWO

As Butler heard the approaching footsteps reluctantly he stepped away from Glenda's embrace. 'Now what?' he said, as someone pounded on the door.

Sally stood outside, breathless and red-faced. 'Captain Butler! Come quickly. You must do something.'

'What is it? What's the matter?'

'They're about to lynch Harry Phillips! And the other one as well, I expect.'

'Oh God!'

Glenda almost laughed at the look on Butler's face. What a dilemma he found himself in! One minute he had been promising Glenda he'd live a normal life, the next he was hearing about a lynch mob. What should he do?

She smiled and gave him a push. 'Put your boots on and go.'

'Are you sure?'

'Yes. This sort of thing can't be allowed to happen.'

'You two girls stay here. Lock yourselves in.'

'Don't worry about us.'

And without a backward glance, Butler took off for the jailhouse.

Phillips stood in the middle of the cell, facing the mob, a contemptuous sneer twisting his lips. If anyone expected him to act scared, to plead for his life, to cry or confess, they were mistaken. Harry wasn't scared. He'd realized long ago that his life meant little to him. That he was going to lose it here and now at the hands of an enraged mob in a one-horse town was no big deal. The only thing that annoyed him was that because his hands were still secured behind him he had no chance to take any of the bastards with him.

As one man undid the cell, Old Bart intoned, 'Harry Phillips, you have been tried and found guilty of crimes committed in the town of Sweetwater Crossing and are hereby condemned to die.'

'Oh for Chrissakes!' Phillips said in disgust.

'Have you got anything to say?'

'Yeah, but you bunch of snivelling, no-account sonsofbitches wouldn't want to hear it.'

'Get him!'

The door opened, the men surged forward, all around Phillips, all over him, kicking, punching, their anger made worse by the fact that he laughed at them.

Jarrod could tell from the shouts and yells that the men had decided to storm the jail and take Harry out. Not that they would have to do much storming; there was neither a lawman nor a good lock to stop them.

'Come on, let's get on with it,' Old Bart said. 'We agreed no unnecessary violence.'

A couple of the others picked up Phillips from the floor and he was dragged out of the cell and through the office. As they emerged on to the sidewalk, Butler stepped up in front of them.

'Stop this at once!' he ordered.

Old Bart pushed his way to the front. 'Cap'n, this ain't nothin' to do with you. This man has been properly tried and convicted. . . .'

'Yeah, and now we're goin' to hang the bastard!'

There was some laughter at this, but not much, because what they were doing was serious business.

'He must be handed over to the law, properly tried. . . .'

'What law?' Old Bart used the same argument against Butler that had been used against him. 'There ain't no law here. The bastard killed our deputy.'

'Sheriff Beale will arrive soon. He'll take charge of the situation.'

'We ain't waiting for the sheriff. This bastard killed two of our citizens, shot 'em down giving them no chance.'

'It doesn't matter what he's done, he deserves a proper trial.'

'No, he doesn't. He doesn't deserve anything. And after we've finished with this'un we're goin' to do the same for the other one.'

'Kilkline wasn't involved in the robbery here in town.'

'He's wanted for killing though. Get rid of two pests at the same time,' someone else said, everyone nodding in agreement.

'Oh dear, poor old Jarrod,' Phillips said. 'Couldn't you lynch him first so I can watch?'

'I fought for justice for all.' Butler drew his gun. 'You all know me. I know you. You'll have to go through me to get to him.'

'We don't want that, but we will if we have to.'

All the same there were a few shuffles at the edge of the crowd. No one wanted to get shot. No one wanted to shoot Captain Butler. They might well have been persuaded to give up and go home, except that Phillips took the matter into his own hands.

With a smirk and a pronounced drawl, he said, 'Well, please hurry up and make up your goddamned minds about what you want to do. I'm gettin' real fed up just standing here.'

There were mutters and growls of anger. Phillips had come here to town, killed two men and was now mocking them.

One member of the mob, out of Butler's line of sight, stepped forward and hefted his own gun, hitting Butler on the back of the head. Myles went down with a little groan and lay half on, half off the sidewalk.

'There weren't no call for that,' Old Bart protested and quickly bent down to make sure the man was all right.

'Yeah there was. Let's get the hell on with it.'

'I always knew Union soldiers were goddamn useless,' Phillips sneered and spat at Butler as he went by him.

They pushed Phillips onto the road, a few thumping him at the same time. Suddenly, from somewhere across the way, came several rifleshots, all in quick succession. Bullets hit the earth by the feet of the mob, sending up little spurts of dust. The men came to a confused, startled halt. Some of them aimed their guns, but there was no one to shoot at.

'Oh dear, more complications. Am I never to be hanged?'

'Shut up.'

Lester Peabody came out of the general store, holding up a rifle and ready to fire. He came to a halt, not about to make the same mistake as Butler by getting too close and allowing himself to be bushwhacked. Nor was he about to make conversation. These men weren't his neighbours; if he had to shoot them so be it. He wasn't about to lose a prisoner to a lynch mob. He had his reputation to think about.

'Let him go! Step away! Do it or I shoot.' And to emphasize his words Peabody fired again, the bullet landing precariously close to the feet of Old Bart.

The men stared at Peabody, stared at each other, uncertain and worried. Did this man mean what he said? He certainly looked as if he did. And they knew Peabody wasn't the Eastern greenhorn he appeared. What should they do?

Peabody took a couple of steps closer, raising the rifle again, finger squeezing the trigger. 'Let him go. Now!'

'All right, all right!' Old Bart, who was in direct line of fire, cried.

One man said, 'Are we goin' to let one man stop us?' And he raised his gun. The fact that he was in the middle of the others and considered himself safe didn't help him.

Peabody fired and the man reeled away, shot in the leg, to fall crying and squealing in the road, while everyone else stepped away from him, horror on their faces.

'Back off.' Peabody circled the men, watching for any ill-considered movement. 'I hope for your sakes Captain Butler isn't badly hurt.'

'He's all right.'

'No thanks to you.'

'You shot Pete,' Old Bart accused.

'Only because he took no notice of my warning. And he's not badly hurt either. I'll shoot the rest of you, too, but I think it's over, don't you?'

Old Bart nodded sulkily and indicated to a couple of the others to carry the wounded Pete away. The rest slunk off, anxious now not to be associated with what they'd tried to do.

'I didn't want this.'

Peabody looked at Old Bart and shrugged. 'It's nothing to me whether that's so or not. Now go on, get out of here.'

He waited until he was sure they'd all gone and wouldn't come back before bending down by Butler. 'Myles, are you all right?'

With a groan and holding his head, Myles sat up. 'What the hell? Jesus, my head hurts. Phillips?'

'He's still alive.'

'I salute you.' Phillips gave a little bow in Peabody's direction. 'I thought you was all bluster.'

'Well, now you know differently, don't you? Come on, get back in the cell.'

Butler followed, rubbing his head.

'You should stay here and guard him,' Peabody said. 'If he's left alone the lynch mob might well return, and this time succeed.'

Worried about Glenda, Butler reluctantly agreed.

'I'll relieve you in a couple of hours' time. I want something to eat first. And Mrs Ericson is cooking supper.'

Butler looked at Peabody with suspicion in his eyes. The man was up to something, but he couldn't think what. He'd made it clear that he wanted to take Harry Phillips back to Tucson. There was no way he'd leave town, not even with Jarrod, and leave Phillips behind.

As he got to the door, Peabody paused and turned. 'You know, Butler, what this town needs is a new lawman. I reckon you'd make a good deputy, don't you?'

TWENTY-THREE

As Peabody emerged from the jailhouse, Glenda and Sally hurried towards him.

'Mr Peabody, is Myles all right?' Glenda asked anxiously.

'Yes. He's inside. And there wasn't any lynching.' She could hear the whole story from Butler.

'Thank God.' Glenda pushed by Peabody and went into the jail.

Sally stood watching him, hands on her hips. 'Will I see you later?'

'Maybe.'

'Good.'

But Peabody had the feeling that after what he was about to do he wouldn't be very popular with anyone in Sweetwater Crossing, not even Sally. Captain Butler was the hero in this town, not him.

By the time he'd eaten supper at Mrs Ericson's, it was dark. And the streets were quiet. The members of the mob had gone home and so had everyone else.

That suited Peabody. He didn't want any witnesses to stop him. Putting on his bowler hat, he left the general store. Instead of going to the jailhouse to relieve Butler, he went down to the stagecoach-line office.

'What's happening?' Jarrod asked, when he opened the door.

'There's nothing for you to worry about.'

'What are you doing?' Jarrod was most surprised because Peabody was undoing the handcuffs. He was also wary. What was the man up to?

'You're free to go.'

'What? What is this? Some sort of trick? If you can't have me the army ain't about to, so you're going to let me get out of the door and then shoot me for trying to escape? Right?'

'Wrong. Completely and utterly wrong. Look, Kilkline, I'll have enough trouble on my hands taking Phillips back to Tucson, without coping with you as well. Moreover, I don't want to hang around while the army decides your fate or until Sheriff Beale gets here and maybe disputes my right to Phillips.'

'So you're letting me go? I don't believe it. Why?'

Peabody letting his heart rule his head twice in one day – no, Jarrod certainly didn't believe that! He didn't know about the redheaded girl and the fact that her words about fairness had played upon Peabody's mind over the last few days.

'You saved the lives of the posse. You saved me. At

risk to your own life.' Even so, Peabody felt sure he was going to regret this when he came to his senses, but right now he didn't know what else to do.

'Do I thank you?' Jarrod asked.

'No. I doubt if I'm doing you any favours. I reckon you'll have quite enough to contend with once the army gets here and starts after you. And Butler will be coming for you too.'

'You think he'll bother?'

'Yes. You see the next time you see him he'll be wearing a deputy's badge and I think our good captain is so used to doing his duty that he's unlikely to want to let you get away. And, of course, once I've taken Phillips to the authorities in Arizona I'll be tracking you again, too.'

'Jesus! It don't sound like I've got much of a future.'

'You haven't. I'm giving you the chance to slip off but my advice would be for you to stay here and take your chances with the army or forever be looking over your shoulder.'

'I'd rather always be looking over my shoulder, than trust the Union Army.'

'Suit yourself. There's a horse ready down at the livery and some supplies in the saddle-bags. You'd better hurry before Butler remembers you.'

If Jarrod had looked back as he hurried to the livery stable he would have seen Lester Peabody standing on the corner, watching him; but he didn't look back.

He was free to ride away again. Free, for the moment, from the threat of both Lester Peabody and Harry Phillips; even if he wasn't free from the goddamned Yankee army or a Union captain with a new star on his vest.

But, what the hell, he decided he'd take his chances in the hills.